PRINCE ISIDORE

Illustrated by
FELIKS TOPOLSKI

METHUEN

PRINCE ISIDORE

A Novel

by
HAROLD ACTON

METHUEN

First published in 1950

CATALOGUE NO. 95/U

PRINTED IN GREAT BRITAIN

TO

MY GALLANT FRIEND

CHRISTOPHER SYKES

INTRODUCTION

EDWARD GIBBON observed in the eighteenth century that the inhabitants of Naples "seem to dwell on the confines of paradise and hell-fire." This impression persists, perhaps even more strenuously, with observers to-day.

The hell-fire aspect was aggravated by the recent world war. But apart from the war's depredations, so feelingly described by Mr. John Horne Burns in "The Gallery," in Naples, of all cities most human, blithe beauty has always been very close to terror. The graceful shore was moulded by volcanic agencies. Vesuvius continues to dominate it: in defiance of its perpetual menace, a vast population swarms along the curving coast, over the climbing terraces and tiers of houses on spurs of semicircular hills. The character of this population has been influenced by the lava in the fertile soil, and by the serene—*Vieni sul mar*—expanse of pure sapphire water. Neapolitan passions are as reckless as their pleasures, and both find expression in song that seldom ceases, day or night.

"A blend of humour and melancholy," writes one of them, "they submit to everything, shrugging their shoulders resignedly and murmuring the fatalistic phrase, which contains all their philosophy, '*Non c'è che fa*'—'There's nothing to be done about it.' "

With Vesuvius and the ruins of Pompeii so near, both destroyer and destroyed suave in the usual sunshine, this attitude is comprehensible. Since Virgil's time the landscape has often been transformed by local eruptions: the crater called Monte Nuovo was belched into being in the sixteenth century, and the Lucrine Lake, once an imposing sheet of water, was reduced to landscape garden dimensions. There is no defence against such caprices of Dame Nature. But against the malign influence of individuals men have gradually forged a whole armoury of weapons, which have been catalogued exhaustively by Valletta, W. W. Story, Dumas *père*, Elworthy, and others. The most efficacious and ubiquitous is the horn.

"Chance," wrote Stendhal, "took me this morning to the home of Don Nardo, the most famous lawyer in Naples. In his ante-room I found an immense bull's horn, perhaps ten feet high; it stuck out of the floor like a nail. I suppose it must be made of three or four bull's horns. It is a lightning conductor for *jettatura*— the spell an ill-disposed person can cast over you with

viii

a look. 'I am aware of the absurdity of the custom,' Don Nardo said to me when he was showing me out, 'but what will you? A lawyer is liable to make enemies, and this horn reassures me.' "

"I am aware of the absurdity of the custom"—so say all. But the fixed belief in a power of evil ejaculated upon any object it beholds has not yet been eradicated. Even amongst the enlightened it still exists, though it may not be acknowledged. Horns of coral and other materials are worn as amulets, on necklaces, bracelets, watch-chains and what not. Even mules and donkeys wear them. For all are equally vulnerable to the Evil Eye.

Jettatura, by which this blighting fascination is known in Naples, is the substantive of the verb *jettare*, to cast a spell by touch, word or look, or by all three combined. The look, however, is the most penetrating, persistent and potent of the trio.

That an evil influence should dart from the eyes of envious or angry persons seems logical; the illogical part of it is that a glance may perpetrate injury without the glancer's consent and even against his will. According to learned authorities on the subject, fascination is of two kinds, moral and natural. The moral kind is exerted by will power; the natural is unconscious and therefore the most to be dreaded.

The obvious *jettatore* can be recognized by certain characteristics. He is lean, sallow, morose, with a hooked nose and hollow eyes under heavy brows, and he is wont to wear thick spectacles. But the subtlest are seldom obvious: they may be plump and pink and

merry, yet nothing they touch or scrutinize will prosper.
Catastrophe follows in their wake.

Without harbouring any cruel design and from no
apparent fault of his own, the most virulent *jettatore* has
the attribute of bringing misfortune on others wherever
he goes. At its very mildest the spell he casts is "sus-
pensive": he hinders your plans by making you miss
an engagement or a train. Anybody suspected of this
proclivity is shunned like the plague, for every obscure
ailment and unaccountable disaster is habitually
credited to him or her. Upon his or her appearance in a
crowded street, everybody takes to flight. There is a rush
into shops, down side alleys, anywhere out of range. . . .

When horns are not available, the repetition of the word "horn" in a forceful tone, or the gesture of the horned hand, will occasionally suffice. The female fascinator or *jettatrice* is said to be less pernicious than the male of the species; however, Jorio tells a pertinent anecdote in his *Mimica degli Antichi*, which illustrates to what lengths a credulous *Napoletana* will go when confronted with a feminine evil eye. "Observing that another lady whom she believed to be a *jettatrice* was highly praising the handsomeness of her husband, and especially of his well-formed thighs and legs, she wished to have recourse to the horn. Not having at hand the grand preservative, nor being able to supply it openly by gesture, furthermore, not believing the word *corno* to be sufficient, she pretended to have need of a handkerchief. She therefore put her hand into her husband's pocket, and there made the *mano cornuta*. Then, with the points of her index and little fingers well extended, she began to stab the thigh-bone of her husband with such force as if she wanted to drill a hole in it; indeed, if she did not pierce it, it was only because she could not. Nor did she leave off her preventive operation until the presumed *jettatrice* turned her talk in another direction. Neapolitan ladies wear little horned hands of various materials suspended at the end of a necklace, which is ordinarily hidden in the bosom; but whenever a person appears who is suspected of being a *jettatore*, the hand goes quickly to the necklace and the amulet is brought out, dangling in the direction considered necessary. As etiquette does not permit this to be done openly in society, they pretend to be adjusting the kerchief, but the fact remains that they seek to make sure of, and touch if possible, the *gran preservatore del fascino*."

In an atmosphere permeated by this superstition, the mind inevitably pins a mishap on to some recent encounter and probes, detective-wise, for the human agent of its ache or pain. *Jettatura* is always floating in the air, and you cannot be too careful. By nurturing this suspicion, you may foist almost any disaster on the last person spoken to before its occurrence. This becomes a mental habit. When ill-luck is definitely anticipated the stage is set for it, so to speak, and the curtain has risen. You conjure the ill-luck in advance.

W. W. Story[1] relates several stories of reputed *jettatori* of which this is the reasonable explanation, such as that of Marchese B——, who called on a party of friends as they were about to set off in carriages for a picnic. "At once there was confusion and dismay. Some wished to put it off altogether, others thought it would have a very ugly look in his eyes and that they had better go, after taking all possible precautions to avert the *jettatura*; and so it was decided. The gaiety, however, was at an end; everyone expected ill-luck, and so it happened. They had hardly gone a mile when the horses of one of the carriages bolted, upset the vehicle, and so frightened and hurt those who were in it that they refused to go farther, and the picnic was given up."

Not a few harmless innocents have gained this notoriety owing to an unhappy coincidence or series of

---

[1] *Castle St. Angelo and the Evil Eye*, London, 1877.

coincidences. No matter how amiable their intentions, they create a flurry of panic. By auto-suggestion merely—from the shock of encountering a reputed *jettatore*—some accident is bound to follow. And even now Naples glories in the serio-comic legends of certain fascinators. The Neapolitan Bourbons were firm believers in them, and there was one priest whom King Ferdinand I was always particular to avoid. For years the King had kept him at bay, but on January 2nd, 1825, he was at last persuaded to grant him an audience instead of going to Caserta for a day's shooting, which was his customary excuse.

"The King's first impulse is always a right one," wrote a contemporary historian, "but he is afraid he may be mistaken, gives ear to representations, and lets himself be led, or gets bored." Canon Ojori, the priest in question, was anxious to present his last published book to the sovereign. The audience lasted two hours, and before his departure the Canon left his book, with many prayers for the King's prosperity. King Ferdinand must have forgotten to provide himself with a horn, for he did not long survive the interview. In fact, he died the day after. The doctors attributed his death to a stroke of apoplexy, but other Neapolitans knew better.

Passing from the sublime to the ridiculous, we have Abate Filippo di Martino's elegy on the decease of a venerable parrot, owing to the fatal glance of a professor of jurisprudence.

But of all the fascinators in this line, none has surpassed Prince Isidore Pizzofalcone—I conceal his

true surname in deference to his living descendants. The following pages are intended as a simple, unvarnished record of the Prince's career. Dumas *père* has been my predecessor in his sparkling book of travel *Le Corricolo*, but my narrative, which repeats his in many respects, has been gathered from several additional sources. It is possible that Dumas saw the Prince in his ripe old age and that his hasty departure from Naples was prompted by that meeting rather than by difficulties with the police, who had identified him despite his incognito. This may explain why his account suffers from a lack of sympathy with the Prince as a human being.

Prince Isidore Pizzofalcone was a man more sinned against than sinning, and I have essayed to depict him in his undoubted pathos, to be faithful rather than entertaining in the process. Although here and there I omit some tendentious passages, condense others and disguise a few names, I have interpolated nothing. While I cannot claim that it is complete, for a chronicle of all the disasters which have been traced directly and indirectly to Prince Isidore would fill a bookshelf of bulky volumes, I can at least vouch for its historical accuracy.

After a careful consideration of the Prince's chequered life, I am sure the reader will agree that we might fittingly apply to him as epitaph a paraphrase of Leopardi's words: "This was a noble nature: one that dared to lift up its mortal eyes and face our common fate, and detracting naught from truth, frankly admitted the evil that is our lot."

Requiescat in pace!

THE Princess Pizzofalcone had been shrieking and groaning for days in her stately, canopied bed.

The bluer the blood the more painful the pangs of birth, as everybody knows, but the unhappy Princess had been in labour for over a week, as if the extreme Radicals had bribed fate to punish her for her exalted family tree. Her physician forbade the use of sedatives, lest it impair the health of the future babe. "The poor mother doesn't seem to count," she complained. "What if I should succumb? San Gennaro and all the blessed saints take pity on me. I'm bursting, I can't breathe!" She emitted a long-drawn wail, more akin to that of a werewolf than of a human being.

All the women in the palace shuddered to the marrow of their bones. The shrill screams from the bedroom of honour vibrated through the entire structure and unsettled the stoutest nerves. The very scullions in the kitchen stirred their pots with a woebegone air. Nobody could sleep soundly at night, for it was like the recurrent echoes of a torture.

But the physician remained adamant. No sedatives. Let the shrieks tire themselves out; they were but natural, he said, under the circumstances, and good exercise for lungs in a horizontal posture.

Marietta, the family midwife, would not agree. Why, her Highness had had no trouble at all when Prince Hercules was born! He had slipped into the world ever so gently, without a murmur on either side. There must be something amiss this time. It was intolerable to see her dear mistress in such misery. She crept out and purchased some laudanum on the sly, but the doctor caught her in the act of administering it and threatened to prosecute her as a poisoner. Her vociferous protestations added to the pandemonium while the Princess cried: "Oh San Gennaro and all the saints, I'm bursting."

"That is not an unusual sensation," drawled the doctor, "under the circumstances."

"You mean it is not usual," said Marietta. "As yet there's no sign whatever of the infant. I'm beginning to think that her Highness is swollen with something else. It looks more like the dropsy to me. Or one of those barbarous diseases from Africa brought over by the pirates."

"Nonsense, woman. A midwife ought to know better. This time it may either be twins or triplets."

"All I know is, the condition of her Highness isn't normal. I witnessed the birth of Prince Hercules. His head was enormous, but it couldn't have popped out more easily. We had another doctor on that occasion, the unrivalled Pacchioni. He stood at the very top of his profession."

"Why was he not consulted, then?"

"He has joined the great majority, God rest his soul." The words were uttered piously, but her glance was venomous. Had Prince Pizzofalcone been in Naples, another physician might have been summoned, but the Prince had been sent on an embassy to Tuscany, and during his absence the midwife could not act on her own initiative. In the meantime, the Princess writhed in agony. She could digest nothing; with the utmost effort, she could swallow a trickle of syrup.

Finally, when the infant reached the outer world after an interminable and most complicated delivery, the Princess was denied the consolation of seeing her younger son. With the child's first breath the Princess breathed her last.

"It is hardly an auspicious beginning for the babe," said the midwife. "Either his future will be very, very black . . ."

"Or very, very rosy," said the physician.

"I fear this bereavement will break the Prince's heart."

"If I read him aright, he will marry again," said the doctor. "He is the uxorious type of philanderer.

3

And the Tuscan Court abounds in feminine beauty. There's plenty of fish in the sea, as the saying goes."

"Florence is not on the sea," Marietta retorted. "The sea is with us, in Naples. Even so, I doubt if the Prince will remarry. In his peculiar way he worshipped the Princess."

"Time fortifies friendship, but weakens love, as some philosopher observed."

"So deep a love as the Prince's will take an age to heal. Little Hercules will keep the wound open. He is the living image of his mother."

"You talk like an old spinster," said the doctor. "A *galantuomo* of the Prince's temperament is bound to find another wife, and that soon. It is axiomatic."

"Heaven be praised, all men are not like you!"

The palace was plunged into mourning and, since womenfolk predominated, the new-born infant's cries were inaudible above the chorus of lamentation.

On receiving this dismal news, Prince Pizzofalcone returned post-haste to Naples. He regretted his wife too poignantly to embrace his second offspring— regretted her all the more because he had been unfaithful since the first day of his marriage. He beat his breast at the memory of his infidelities. Too late, alas, too late! He shuddered at the sight of the babe, so harmless in appearance, yet guilty of a cruel matricide. A flash of indignation darted through the tears that glistened in his eyes, and he wished the creature dead instead of its mother.

He wept long and loud as he sat with the livid corpse in his nuptial chamber. "She shall remain as beautiful

4

as she was in life," he said, and ordered her maid to rouge her lips and cheeks. But the effect was even more ghastly when she was laid in an open coffin, her face uncovered, and carried through the streets. The huge church had been draped in black with designs of skulls and crossbones. It was without light except for four tapers standing at the corners of a raised platform on which she lay, surrounded by cowled monks chanting the *De Profundis*. The widower had devised every means of increasing the horror of her death, and had succeeded so well that his hair turned white though he was under thirty.

The Prince was too distracted to present himself at Court. King Ferdinand would never have noticed this, since he was engaged in his favourite pastime of shooting pheasants on the island of Procida. But it was the Queen who ruled, and Maria Carolina was highly incensed with the envoy to her son-in-law, the Grand Duke of Tuscany, for absenting himself without leave. She suspected him, like so many of her subjects, of Jacobin tendencies. When the Prince had mastered his grief sufficiently to pay his respects at Caserta, their Majesties turned stiff backs on him without a word, and he found himself cold-shouldered by the entire Court in consequence. Though he pleaded domestic tragedy in justification, his eloquence fell on deaf ears. He was dismissed from his post so curtly that he could entertain scant hope of being reinstated.

This disgrace, on top of his bereavement, quite deadened any glimmer of affection for his younger son. The Prince would not even attend his baptism. Yet the babe was a bonny one, "a cherub that only wanted wings," said Marietta as she dandled him on her knee before a pitying audience. Why blame the poor mite for its mother's death? Personally she threw the blame on the bungling doctor.

A vigorous peasant *balia* was engaged to nurse the child. No sooner had his tiny fingers touched her bosom than her milk supply turned sour. Isidore, as he had been christened, grew purple and had convulsions, while the nurse protested that she had never had such an accident in all her long experience. Besides his elder brother Hercules, had she not suckled innumerable males, including an octogenarian bishop, to health and strength?

She suspected the interference of a malevolent spirit, but she kept this to herself. Alarmed and mortified, considering her hitherto untarnished record, she resigned her charge to a nanny goat which was brought into the palace as a substitute. Its heavy udders slaked the babe's fierce appetite, and Isidore flourished as if there were a blood relationship between them. He skipped and hopped before he learned to toddle and retained a goatish bounce in after life, thanks to which he could be recognized a mile away. The Prince his father kept him out of sight and lavished all his affection on his firstborn.

Unlike Hercules at the same age, Isidore had no mother's arms to cling to, no bosom to nestle in, no tender love to cradle him to sleep. He had nothing, in fact, but the nanny goat's swollen udders. Yet he continued to thrive in seclusion, set apart from other

6

children. As he approached boyhood he might have been frozen by this inhuman solitude and neglect. Happily for him, he did not feel wronged, for he had a modest disposition and expected little from life—so little, indeed, that on hearing that the poisonous hemlock was a sort of grass which brought death, he gorged himself with grass out of the garden, in the belief that it might contain that dormitive. He had no clear notion what death was, but already he had more curiosity about it than about its apparent alternative. Existence at home was featureless. His father decided that the most convenient form of riddance was to send him to be educated at a remote seminary, after which he could enter a remoter monastery. Isidore, even had he been informed of this plan for his future, was too young to raise any objection.

On the day he entered the seminary all the other boys in his class succumbed to an epidemic of whooping cough, and it was noted with surprise that the new-comer remained immune. He prospered as by magic, precocious in many things, and soaring rapidly in every branch of study, a mystic equivalent, perhaps, of the affection he had been denied at home. This did not render him popular with his class-mates, but they regarded him with a certain awe. They dared not bully him for his bouncing gait, for he had a strange fascination of the eye which could be frightening, particularly after sunset. His eyes seemed to flash of a sudden in their sockets, and he only had to fix his gaze on a person to make him feel uncomfortable. The peculiar intensity of his look escaped definition. It was as if he had been provided with double pupils, and two pairs of bulging eyes superimposed on each other. Thus he made neither friends nor enemies, and never a practical joke, a lark or a scrape, disturbed the monotony of his studious routine. He won most of the prizes without apparent effort. Only once did he fail to win the first prize, and then the winner stumbled on climbing the steps of the podium and fractured his skull.

Remote as the seminary was from Naples, there were pleasant country houses scattered about the neighbourhood, and on Sunday walks Isidore sometimes caught glimpses of ladies in gaudy coaches accompanied by gallants on horseback, gay parties setting out for a rural picnic or excursion. Each lovely form was tinged by his fancy in hues even lovelier. He would peer into the distance until the vision faded, little guessing that the coach would ultimately break down. Not without a sigh, he compared his condition with theirs, which he pictured as one of continuous revelry. He dreamed of them at night; by day they disturbed his study of Aristotle and the Sacred Fathers. Knowing nothing of any kind of love, his mind dwelt fervently on images.

This tendency was increased by a trifling incident. He had picked up a scented glove which had been dropped from a barouche on the highway, and, on restoring it to its flamboyantly feminine owner, he kissed her hand. The hand was so milky white and meltingly soft that his lips clung hungrily to its surface with a persistence more ardent than usual on such occasions.

The lady burst out laughing. "For a priestling you

seem pretty forward," she remarked. "I'm afraid you have made an error in your vocation."

"I could kiss your hand for ever," he boldly rejoined. "Nay, more, I could kiss your arms, your shoulders, your lips, your eyes. . . ."

"You saucy boy! Is that what they teach you at the seminary?" She laughed again, disclosing two rows of such pearly teeth that his knees were all of a tremble. The musical echoes of her laughter echoed within him long after that brief encounter. He was haunted by the voluptuous apparition, which prevented him from deriving pleasure or profit from the banal circumstances that gave pleasure or profit to others, and turned his youth into a long, exhausting dream. Until then he had had wistful cravings for the cool little choristers swinging censers and singing *Te Deums* in the seminary chapel. Their pure white surplices were now replaced by satin bodices and crinolines, swelling and undulating in the scirocco of his desire.

He tried to curb himself by a system of moral and intellectual cold water, meagre diet and excessive exercise, but the dream persevered. His expression became so ecstatic that his teachers began to mistake him for a mystic. He rose in the dawn to ruminate on the pleasures of the outside world. He retired at night still glowing with secret passion—he knew not exactly for whom—and within his soul a voice cried out for amorous annihilation.

He imagined himself drowning in an amethyst lake while the bosoms of swans floated gracefully overhead. The bubbles of his ebbing breath exploded like stars around him, and the smooth white swans became breasts of sirens tipped with coral, crushing him slowly with a soft and silent pressure. He sank into an oozy bed of water-weeds and when he awoke his thighs were wet, which seemed to prove the truth of his recent experience. Yet he was free from physical ailments and continued to pass his examinations *summa cum laude.* In the opinion of his examiners, he was dangerously clever for his age. All of them, however, were afflicted with unaccountable headaches during the *viva voce.* Their temples began throbbing at the very first question, and the throbbing did not subside until Isidore withdrew.

In the meantime, great changes were happening in Naples. Reports of them reached the seminary and excited the students with a patriotic frenzy entirely new to them. Day and night the arsenals were busy: new ships of war were being built for the royal fleet and munitions of every kind were being collected; large levies of recruits were being raised and volunteers were hired from distant parts. For the storm of revolution had burst over France, and the Neapolitan Bourbons identified the cause of the French Bourbons with their own. When her sister Marie Antoinette was guillotined, the Queen persuaded King Ferdinand to prepare for hostilities with France. It was announced with due solemnity that the Archbishop of Naples would bless the banners of the recently formed regiments in the Duomo.

As the ceremony was unusual and the Cathedral could not accommodate the entire population, only the most prominent colleges and seminaries had the privilege of sending representatives. Among the distinguished students who had the honour of being selected was young Don Isidore. For him this was a wonderful reward, a golden day in his drab calendar.

It was seven years since he had last set foot in Naples, and the glittering bay seemed to greet him with outstretched arms, holding promise of future delights. Though he could not linger gazing on the scene, he thanked Heaven for so sumptuous a gift, and with blood effervescing he entered the dim Cathedral. The ceremony opened to the pealing of bells and the melodious thunder of two pompous organs. Amid clouds of incense, the Archbishop blessed each banner in sonorous Latin. Isidore could discern his father near the high altar, a cadaverous figure in black. Oh for a friendly glance of recognition! But the Prince was absorbed in telling his rosary, looking neither to right nor to left.

After the benediction all banners were raised in procession to file out of the Cathedral. While the first one was passing Isidore, its bearer collapsed on the pavement. Isidore rushed forward to his assistance, but the poor fellow was beyond human aid. He had evidently died of a stroke. With exemplary presence of mind, Isidore made himself master of the situation. He seized the fallen banner, and hoisting it with a martial air, he shouted: "Long live the King!" The loyal crowd repeated this cheer in deafening unison.

This episode made a deeper impression than the

preceding ceremony on those who witnessed it. It brought a tear of pride to Prince Pizzofalcone's eye, and he had a momentary impulse to embrace his outcast son. But this was soon checked by recalling the dead wife to whom he had been so unfaithful.

Three months later the Neapolitan army had crumbled at every point of contact with the French. The two generals San Filippo and Micheroux had run away almost within sight of the enemy at Fermi, and the former had been shot in the arm by one of his own sergeants while galloping off. Many had run thirty miles without stopping. In seven combats ten thousand were taken prisoners; their banners had been captured; their cannons, ammunition and equipment were abandoned helter-skelter. The King himself fled from the field of battle in civilian disguise. And when his strongholds in the Abruzzi fell like ninepins before the Republican generals, the entire royal family escaped from a back door of the palace under cover of darkness and set sail for Sicily on Nelson's *Vanguard*. So stormy was the passage that Prince Alberto, the youngest of the royal children, died in Emma Hamilton's arms before reaching Palermo.

Having graduated from the seminary, Isidore entered the monastery of Camaldoli, gloomily expecting to spend the rest of his life there. The day after he moved into this establishment, an edict was promulgated by the new Republican government suppressing religious communities and confiscating all the vast estates belonging to the Orders of Saint Bernard and Saint Benedict. But Isidore was still a younger son, and none the richer for that. There seemed no alternative but to pursue an ecclesiastical career.

His father's confessor had induced that inexorable man to relent in one respect: he allowed Isidore a lodging on the top floor of his palace, provided that he did not trespass in other parts of the building. They seldom crossed each other's paths, and when they did the Prince pretended not to see him. He had sent his elder son Hercules to travel abroad with a learned tutor, to avoid contact with Isidore rather than to improve his mind by seeing the world. He relied on Hercules to uphold the glory of his house, and he was determined that he should take no risks. Nothing was too good for Hercules, who had developed into a spirited young man with a keen sense of his own valour. The whole of the family fortune was already settled on him, and with his muscular prowess and polished manners he cut a fine figure wherever he went, and made innumerable conquests.

A period of chaos followed the King's flight to Sicily. Naples was divided against itself, and terrorized by mobs of *lazzaroni*, those sturdy beggars named after Lazarus, whom the monarch had ever paternally indulged. Their devotion to the absent Ferdinand now burst forth with destructive intensity. Prince Pignatelli, the acting regent, lost his nerve. The valuable frigates and warships in the harbour were burned; the gunpowder stored in the Torretta was destroyed, and the newly formed national guard could not prevent the *lazzaroni* from opening the prisons and letting loose a horde of malefactors. Then Pignatelli fled after his monarch, and the rabble ran riot. There was pillage and arson everywhere, and even the royal palace was sacked. But the French and San Gennaro, whose relics were exposed to the masses, restored some semblance of order. General Championnet persuaded the people of the futility of further resistance. He swore to respect the persons and property of Neapolitan citizens, their Catholic heritage, and their patron Saint, to whom rich offerings were brought, escorted by two companies of grenadiers as a guard of honour. While marching through the crowded streets, the grenadiers shouted, "All honour to San Gennaro!" The fickle populace shouted back: "Long live the French!" And when Naples was proclaimed the Parthenopean Republic, the immense population sauntered about as if it were Holy Thursday, drinking and fraternizing with the French soldiery in the taverns. Rank and fashion also vied in showing hospitality to the French officers.

Horrified by the fate of his friends, the Duca della Torre and Don Clemente Filomarino, two harmless old gentlemen who had been strapped to chairs, shot and burned by the rabble on the Marinella, Prince Pizzofalcone retired to a distant castle, leaving Isidore in the city with a few veteran retainers. For the next few weeks Isidore basked in comparative freedom, strolling through Naples in a three-cornered hat, a black cloak and violet stockings, in quest of romantic adventure. He dallied away his afternoons on the Chiaia and the Toledo, which was then the largest and finest thoroughfare in Europe. But the adventure he sought eluded him; and freedom soon palls in a city without friends.

The abolition of the law of primogeniture was one of the first measures of the new government. This deprived Hercules of half his large revenue, but to Isidore it came as a blessing undisguised. He was heartily sick of the profession imposed on him. Having no contempt for the vanities of a world of which he knew so little, he was resolved to rush headlong into the life of a fashionable young man about town.

His first act was to summon the best tailor, hatter, hosier, and shoemaker in Naples. He ordered fifty embroidered coats, looped and braided, in varying shades of blue and purple and maroon, cut open in front and sewn with jewelled buttons, besides fifty double waistcoats to set off his laced shirts, cravats and ruffles. He chose the lightest and tightest of pantaloons, favouring primrose yellow. It was the latest vogue to wear them *collant* to the thighs and legs, with silk stockings to silhouette a shapely calf, and pointed shoes so tiny that they pinched. To wriggle in and out of such pantaloons without splitting them at the seams was a problem which caused Isidore acute concern each time he dressed and undressed. For his hips were his capital feature. What would he do in an amorous emergency? But he decided to follow the mode—though it cramped his style and entailed some stiff gymnastics. As for his hats, they were cocked and laced with gold.

Since the chief amusement of Naples was the Corso, when the ladies drove out with six, and often with eight horses, he bought himself a magnificent equipage, a high-sprung cabriolet of turquoise blue, lined with velvet, spangled with silver stars within and without, and enamelled with his family escutcheon. His horses were the largest and strongest in any Neapolitan stable, with manes and tails as fine as flax, of a great length, like solid waves; their harness was of blue and silver, and the ornament that covered the crest of their manes represented rows of convolvuluses formed of the same materials, most delicately woven. On their heads they bore white ostrich feathers and artificial flowers.

Isidore's next ambition was to secure a suitable mistress, and this was less easy to realize.

Unfortunately for him, in so compact if not exclusive a society as that of Naples, republican or royal, it was inevitable that alarming rumours should circulate about Don Isidore. All Neapolitans dreaded the Evil Eye, before whose fatal glance all men are equal.

Isidore was reputed to possess it, though he had none of the conspicuous characteristics of the *jettatore*.

Certainly his eyes were peculiar, but his person was plump and suave. He retained a cherubic air of infancy.

The accidents which had accompanied his sporadic appearances in public were remembered against him, however, and he was shunned without having a suspicion of the cause. Those who encountered him were alert to make horns with their hands, by extending the first and little fingers and folding the others firmly against the thumb, even when coral horns and other talismans of classic origin were dangling from their waistcoat pockets.

A few agnostics scoffed at these sinister rumours, and foremost among these was the Countess of Mirafiore, the reigning toast of the new régime in Naples.

WITH the arrival of the Republican French, scepticism had become rampant in superstitious Naples. What were called "French principles" had infiltrated into fashionable society, especially that portion of it which professed allegiance to Napoleon. The young Countess of Mirafiore, who was as pretty and musical as her name, had a passion for everything Parisian, from *bidets* to political ideas. She preferred airing her volatile opinions in French, though she never succeeded in pronouncing the language correctly.

All Gauls were assured of a warm welcome in her *salon*, and a few were even admitted to the warmer favours of her bedroom. Her mansion, one of the most attractive on the Chiaia, became a stronghold of

Republicanism. General Championnet was in the habit of spending the afternoon in her apartments and often of dispatching state business there, sometimes into the smallest hours. The new red, blue and yellow flag fluttered from her balcony, and a tree of liberty was planted in her courtyard.

Her penchant for equality and fraternity, besides liberty, did not deter the Countess from spending a revenue in dress, and her rooms were positively regal. The grand saloon was lined with mirrors, on which trellises of foliage, birds and flowers were painted in the rococo style of Pillement, twisting and twining over the pools of glass. She called it her rustic arbour.

"I am only a little country bird," she said. "I feel quite lost in the metropolis. But among these leaves and flowers I am at home and can chirrup to my heart's content."

Here she received her visitors and punctuated their chatter, never losing sight of herself in one of the mirrors as she turned now and then to address them in a pose that was anything but pastoral.

"How is it, madam," inquired a French visitor, "that I see no horns in any of your apartments?"

"What do you mean, sir?"

"So far I have not entered a house in Naples without finding a pair of horns on one of the walls. At first I thought they must either be emblems or warnings to cuckolds, for they were too numerous to be trophies of any other kind of chase. But I hear they are lightning conductors for *jettatura*. Have you no fear of the Evil Eye, madam?"

"Of course not. How could you think me so old-fashioned?"

"But surely you believe in fascination? The word may have lost its meaning but not its power. 'If looks could kill,' we say, forgetting that this is quite possible. And that looks can almost kill, you are a living proof."

"You flatter me, sir, but I have yet to be convinced."

"Have you not read Niccolo Valletta's learned treatise on the subject?"

"I have no time for such rubbish."

"Since coming to Naples I have begun to believe in it, and I am supported by history and archæology. The ancient Egyptians, Hebrews, Greeks and Romans were all familiar with it and took proper precautions. When a person was ill without apparent cause, the Romans exclaimed, '*Mantis te vidit*'—some fascinator has seen you. This fascination was said to be of two kinds, moral and natural. Those who had the moral kind could only practise it by will power, but those in whom it was natural could not help exerting it unconsciously, and they were the most dangerous."

"You look so sensible," said the Countess, "and so contemporary. I am rather disappointed."

"You mean susceptible, madam. Perhaps I am too susceptible to the atmosphere of Naples, the *genius loci*. You make me all the more so."

"I'm sorry if it affects you superstitiously. The Evil Eye is a relic of the bad old past. Let us bury it."

"You cannot bury what is alive and flourishing. Have you not heard of Don Isidore Pizzofalcone?

Wherever he goes he brings calamity. Why, only the other day . . ."

"I don't believe a word of it. He's a very presentable young man. A bit overdressed perhaps, and he has an eccentric walk, but that can soon be remedied by a French dancing master. The poor fellow was brought up at a seminary. I'm glad he has come into some money. The old primogeniture law was monstrously unfair."

"Has Don Isidore ever been inside your house?"

"As a matter of fact, he hasn't. Which reminds me I must do something about it. It's outrageous the way he is treated. Everybody runs from him like a gaggle of startled geese. I should like to teach them a lesson."

"Charity begins at home," remarked a wag. "Would you challenge this superstition by inviting him to your palace?"

The Countess flushed. "An admirable proposition," she retorted. "I shall hold a gala reception in his honour. That should put a stop to this nonsense once and for all."

News of the challenge spread like wildfire through the city. At first those who had been invited were reluctant to accept. They remembered how lustily Isidore had shouted, "Long live the King!" at the ceremony of blessing the banners in the Cathedral. True, the King was still alive, but not in Naples; and after so decisive a defeat his return was most unlikely. Well, well, if they attended the reception they need not be taken by surprise. They could arm themselves with amulets in advance.

The Neapolitans are irrepressibly gregarious. There had been few social entertainments since the King's flight, and when the day of the party came round, curiosity conquered fear. By nine o'clock that evening the guest rooms of the Mirafiore mansion were crowded to full capacity. She had had most of them redecorated in the latest Parisian style, banishing the shelves of Capodimonte and the rows of periwigged ancestors, and introducing stiff-backed chairs and settees, tables and cabinets designed in rebellion against the frills and furbelows of the departed Bourbons. An Egyptian severity of ornament prevailed, which reflected Napoleon's victories in the East. The elaborate stuccoes of her boudoir had been draped in the manner of a military tent, where space is doubly precious. The rose satin drawing-room had been filled with golden eagles, Napoleon's birds. Above the vast bow windows which afforded an uninterrupted panorama of the bay, the cornices of the curtains supported eagles with spread pinions, and eagles supported the console tables where Isis and Osiris, standing on sphinx pedestals, held branching candlesticks.

The guests overflowed through these apartments into the equally decorous garden. Chinese lanterns lit the pergolas and gazebos, and musicians from the San Carlo were grouped in fancy dress under the trees, competing with the nightingales as in a scene by Watteau. At ten o'clock, when the party was in full swing, Don Isidore, "dei Principi Pizzofalcone," was announced.

In a twinkling the festive rooms were hushed to a

stupefied silence. Every eye sought to avoid Isidore's, yet, strained with a horrified attention, could not help focusing his dapper form. Even the irresponsible French officers appeared disconcerted. When they had sufficiently recovered their urbanity, the prime preoccupation of all present was to decide the important question: shall I be spared?

A few forked their fingers, still craning their necks and peering in his direction; and a few beat a hasty retreat.

Considering the flutter he had created, Isidore appeared floridly self-possessed in his costume of plum-coloured velvet. He paused on the threshold of the drawing-room with a seraphic smile, aware that he was a cynosure, but ignorant of the reason. He supposed it must be due to his charm. He had had occasion to admire the shapeliness of his proportions while dressing and had split two pairs of breeches in the process. His fastidious French barber had complimented him on the curls which rose from his forehead in copious clusters.

"What a wonderful wig they would make," he exclaimed. "I could not do better with my tongs in an exceptional flight of fancy, assisted by a magnum of champagne. Your hair looks exquisitely artificial."

"Should it not look natural?" Isidore inquired.

"Nothing fashionable should ever look natural," the barber retorted superciliously. "Fashion should improve on Nature's handiwork."

23

Isidore meditated on the barber's maxim. Who would have guessed, himself least of all, that the callow seminarist was to blossom into so consummate a beau? On further reflection, he concluded that it must be the will of Heaven, as preordained as the metamorphosis of caterpillar into butterfly.

He had surveyed himself in his new rôle with pride and satisfaction. Now that he was being surveyed by others, he was anxious to produce an equally favourable impression.

It is the first step which counts, he remembered; this is my *début* in polite society, a portentous moment in my career. To conceal the thumping of his heart amid the blaze of candelabra, he opened the lid of his snuff-box with the thumb of the hand that carried it, while he delicately took his pinch with two fingers of the other. He had practised the pose until it was quite perfect.

The gesture provoked a mild panic, since a snuff-box was reputed to increase the virulence of the Evil Eye.

"Now we're in for it," muttered a famous magistrate, grasping the coral antlers on his watch-chain. "You mark my words, the mischief is about to begin. This is the prologue."

Just then a trifling accident occurred, but it might have been due to casual clumsiness. A footman carrying a tray of raspberry sherbet tripped over the Countess's poodle, and the contents fell all over the Aubusson carpet. One lady's white dress was bespattered, but no serious damage was done. The lady's cry and the poodle's yapping drew attention to the mishap, and its coincidence with Isidore's arrival made it a matter of general comment.

Isidore took another pinch of snuff and went in search of his hostess, who was strolling in the garden with a coterie of courtiers. "We admire your courage," they told her. "Who else would dare invite the Unmentionable?"

"If you refer to it again you'll annoy me," she said. "I'm determined to vindicate the poor pet."

"He has caused a few casualties already."

"Of what sort, sir? Please do not quiz me."

"A tray of sherbet dropped by a footman, and Signora Gabrieli's dress, which was ruined in consequence—not to mention your Aubusson carpet and your poodle, who cut his paw on a splinter of glass."

"Such accidents are inevitable at all receptions. I'm sorry about the Gabrieli's gown, but with so noble a bosom the damage will hardly be noticed. Had it happened to me, it would have been a tragedy. I have nothing to boast of, apart from my clothes."

Every man within earshot raised his voice in protest. Every protest, based on experience, was sincere. The Countess of Mirafiore's most effective art was to conceal her art, but when she chose to reveal it, the spectacle was dazzling from top to toe. And the perfume she exhaled was unique. It drowned roses and tuberoses alike, and overpowered the botany of her garden.

It was one of those June evenings, so dangerous to virtue, when the heat of Naples is tempered by frivolous breezes from the ocean. The moon had soared over Vesuvius; the Chinese lanterns were multiplied in the sky. One could not doubt the ancient myth that Parthenope had been built over a siren's grave. The spirit of that tempting siren pervaded the lucid stillness of the night, whispering that beauty was transient and meant to be enjoyed. Isidore seemed to be propelled by that spirit, as he wandered among the guests in search of his hostess.

On catching sight of him, the Countess approached Isidore on her attendant's arm. Her courtiers drew back in dismay when he bowed, and, wreathed in smiles, proceeded to kiss her hand. The usual compliments were exchanged, and to prove her contempt for popular superstition, she released the arm of her escort in exchange for Isidore's. Flattered by this public mark of esteem, he exclaimed, with a glance intended to go directly to her heart, "What a triumph, madam! You have bidden me to a celebration on Olympus. I'll warrant it will be the talk of the town for ages."

"You must not exaggerate," she answered coyly. "It is just a little gathering of friends."

"I am overwhelmed. You treat me as if I were the guest of honour. For me it is the night of nights. Everything under heaven contributes to its success, and heaven has given you perfect weather for the occasion. You could not have ordered a more magnificent moon."

"One can see that you have studied rhetoric to some purpose," said the Countess.

Just then an Olympian blast of thunder resounded. A mysterious cloud, invisible till now, burst over the garden in a sudden torrent. Everybody dashed for shelter, some into the stalactite grotto and Chinese pavilion, others into the palace.

Isidore and his hostess were among the latter. More fortunate than the majority, they had escaped a drenching in the nick of time. For the climate to be so cantankerous in June, when Naples is wont to be as dry as Arabia, was incomprehensible even to those who believed in *jettatura*. Nobody would have dreamed of bringing an umbrella. The sinister prestige of Isidore was enhanced. His power extends to the elements, they observed.

The rose satin drawing-room was crammed with card tables for tombola, the baccarat of the day, and other games of chance. Behind the seated players stood their friends and lovers, since such games allowed intervals of social and amorous intrigue. The yellow ball-room was awhirl with dancers. The Countess thought it prudent to decline Isidore's invitation to join him in a quadrille. "I must see that everybody is enjoying himself," she said, "before yielding to selfish pleasures."

"I hope that portends you will dance with me later, madam?"

"You have my arm already, sir. You must give me your moral support."

"I could desire no more glorious privilege," Isidore beamed. While he examined the dancing couples bobbing their heads up and down, a confusion spread among them. They forgot their steps and trod on each other's toes. Something went wrong with the orchestra

too, for the notes became discordant, and soon the music broke down like a mechanical toy. The violinist waved his instrument, explaining that its strings had snapped. He begged for a little patience while he attempted to repair them. The dancers, hot and flustered, retired towards the grand saloon, where supper was served from a monumental buffet. There was a general stampede towards the dishes, and the babel of tongues passed all understanding, in every sense of the word.

Now that the ball-room was clear, Isidore could

take a measure of its splendid dimensions. It was a vast octagon, towards which the other rooms converged, and it was lighted by a colossal chandelier, which had recently arrived from England in a thousand and one separate pieces. These pieces now composed a floating garden of urn-like balusters, curved stems, sockets with scalloped rim, and flat drops of almond or pear-shaped profile with edges cut in a series of shallow bevels. It had never been lighted before, and the slim candle-flames, reflected by myriads of facets of crystal, were multiplied with magical effect, seeming to glitter with far more colours than any rainbow.

Isidore stood gaping at the spectacle of this frozen cascade suspended in mid-air, and then at his ravishing hostess, but the words refused to come at his bidding. He was struck speechless. Exposed to the glare, the Countess was even more seductive, her skin more lustrous, like animated mother-of-pearl.

"What is the matter?" she asked.

"I have never seen such a chandelier. It is a second sun, and you are a second Venus!"

Before she could reply, the elaborate structure came crashing to the floor, where it was shattered in tiny fragments. Fortunately, most of the guests were still at supper and nobody was injured. The Countess sent for torches of pine, which were held aloft by an avenue of flunkeys as soon as the dance could proceed. "Perhaps the light of the torch flames is an improvement," she remarked. "It is certainly more picturesque."

"But somewhat risky all the same," said Isidore. "Pine-wood is very inflammable. Just look at those sparks! Supposing the panelling were to catch fire?"

"I adore risk," she answered tactfully. "Life would be dull without it."

Instinctively, the Countess led him away from the ball-room. The accidents which had followed each other in swift succession might still be due to chance, but she was assailed by private misgivings. In her heart of hearts she began to regret her temptation of Providence. But the sarcasm of her friends, should she betray any backsliding, quite apart from the difficulty of shaking off her troublesome companion, spurred her on to persevere to the bitter end. She concealed her growing alarm, and continued to load him with constrained civilities. She must not judge him too hastily. . . .

The Countess had engaged the most famous primadonna from the San Carlo to crown the evening with purest melody. No one who had not heard Erminia in "Nina Pazza per Amore"—and half Naples had done so—could know of what enchantment the human voice was capable. What a divine soprano! What a God-given power and pitch filling the great opera house to its remotest corner, yet breathed out as in a melting whisper! No *tremolo*, no *sforzando*, but a sound that swelled with the strength of an archangel and the softness of a dove. The range of Erminia was as remarkable as her technique, and to-night she had promised to surpass herself, for among the guests were two rival impresarios, one of whom had invited her to Paris with the highest salary she had yet received.

The dancing stopped, and with frantic applause the guests made way for the massive nightingale. On a raised platform the accompanist was already seated at her harp. As the bulk of Madame Erminia was waddling across the great hall unescorted, Isidore excused himself to his hostess and, with a graceful bow, offered to pilot the prima-donna to her place. After delivering a short speech about "the three phenomenal years during which this constellation of all singing had enthralled fervent audiences at the San Carlo without ever a rift in the luminous harmony," he made a bee-line for his hostess and seized her arm amid a murmur of approbation. Since a few tongues were still wagging, there was a hissing crescendo of hushes.

The harpist plucked a titillating prelude for the tip-toed audience. The prima-donna coughed a perfunctory cough, made an effort to blush through her rouge, and stretching the enormous cupid's bow of her lips, emitted her first note. She had taken a semi-tone too high and plumb in the middle of the fourth beat she broke into a cacophanous quack. The listeners could hardly believe their ears. This was incredible, unheard of! and all hastened to encourage the *diva* with renewed applause. But Erminia pursed her lips and tossed her mane. Never had she suffered so public a mortification. She was aware that her vocal chords were governed by a malign influence which was irresistible. Suspecting that it was a case of *jettatura* which might ruin her future career, she forked her fingers and swept out of the hall.

Isidore ran forward to intercept and plead with her, but before her frown he quailed. She bridled majestically in her rage, and her black eyes glowed at him like fiery coals, hurling sparks of accusation. There could be no doubt that she attributed to him her extra-ordinary attack of hoarseness. All eyes were fixed on the embarrassed hostess and her calamitous guest of honour.

Isidore condoled with the Countess most eloquently. "I suppose all singers have to be temperamental," he said, "but surely Madame Erminia was unreasonably so to-night. From her demeanour one would have almost thought that I was to blame. I wish I could offer to sing in her stead. Upon my soul you inspire me to, but alas, my voice is untrained." His innocence was disarming.

Proud of the privilege of bearing her arm, he seemed determined never to leave it.

The Countess attempted to disengage herself by feigning fatigue. She asked Isidore to accompany her to her boudoir. Draped like a tent and contrasting with the formality of the other apartments, it was adjacent to the ball-room, where the dance was con-tinuing by torchlight. Isidore moved a settee near the door so that while resting his hostess could watch the company. He begged her to be seated and drew up a chair for himself.

"This is the moment I have been waiting for all evening," he said, "nay, all my life. To be alone with you undisturbed—I declare it is my notion of Paradise. I'm beside myself with joy. Dare I, dare I confess that I have fallen deeply in love?"

The Countess looked up with a startled expression

which Isidore interpreted to his advantage. By heaven, she was moved! His words must have hit their mark. . . .

He drew closer, gazing into her eyes, then crack! the two hind legs of the settee collapsed. The Countess was tumbled backwards, overturning a table with a precious Pompeian vase which was sent crashing against a mirror. The latter, now splintered, would bring seven years' bad luck. As for the Countess, she fell to the floor with a bump. Isidore offered to help her to her feet, but she spurned him with a vivacity no longer veneered with tact. In a flash she ran straight to her bedroom and locked the door. There she threw herself on her bed and sobbed hysterically. Her maids undressed her and soothed her with smelling salts.

In the hostess's absence the party could not proceed. The music stopped; the dancers and card players retired, cursing the killjoy but for whom they would have stayed until daybreak.

Isidore paced to and fro outside his hostess's bedroom, beseeching her to issue. Blind to all but his passion, he was determined to linger in the hope that he might yet persuade her. Footmen were still busy sweeping away the debris. They were sleepy and sullen, and their mutterings about the Evil Eye were loud enough for Isidore to hear. But he could hear nothing save the inner voice of love.

An optimist by nature, he was elated by the events of this dramatic evening. From the sudden storm to the shattered chandelier, there had never been a dull moment. It seemed fitting that that crystalline sun should never blaze again, having lighted the Countess in the full bloom of her beauty. And the prima-donna producing that barnyard cackle! He could not help laughing at the memory of her grimaces.

It was a pity that the party had ended prematurely, but perhaps this would allow him another *tête-à-tête*. The escape to the bedroom had probably been a ruse. The Countess might be waiting for the coast to clear before admitting him. That accident in the boudoir might have been premeditated. The more he considered it, the more calculated it seemed. The Countess was so clever! At least she had given him a glimpse that half the gallants of Naples would have envied.

Isidore shivered in a fever of desire at the memory of her pattern under the petticoats. Indeed he had been blessed by Providence. He was speculating on what course of amorous tactics to pursue when a yawning majordomo begged him to observe that the hour was late and that his continued presence hindered him from extinguishing the lights and closing the gates of the palace.

"But I wish to take leave of her Ladyship!" he protested. "I know that she has something particular to tell me."

"Her Ladyship has left orders that she is not to be disturbed on any account."

"Pray inform her that I shall make my bow at her levée." Isidore could no longer insist. The majordomo made horns behind his back. Reluctantly he retired from the palace, as from a thrilling spectacle before the final act.

The morning air was like a transparent cordial.

Vesuvius puffed his pipe in serene content. To prolong the echoes and sensations of the party, Isidore dismissed his carriage and walked homeward along the Chiaia, musing upon the blessings of this life—of the sunshine, and the invigorating breeze from the sea, which wafted the clear tenors of fishermen in their light skiffs; of honourable duties, agreeable excursions and noble deeds; but above all, of the rosy details of the Countess of Mirafiore.

IT was ironical that the freethinking Countess of Mirafiore should have set a seal to Isidore's reputation. Her entertainment had given him a notoriety which it would have taken him years to gain otherwise.

The accidents for which he was made responsible were embellished. A versified account of them, with an engraving on the title-page depicting the collapse of the chandelier, was printed and hawked in every corner of Naples. This alone was enough to terrorize the common folk, with whom the supernatural outweighs the authority of reason. Henceforth he was all but ostracized, and nobody would approach him without the minutest precautions.

36

The Countess's door was closed to him, and his attempts to bribe her retainers were unavailing. This was at first a bitter disappointment, but it dawned on him gradually that he was in love with love. Novelty is essential to youthful spirits, of which Isidore had no lack, and he soon found consolation in the arms of less difficult maidens. Along the Sorrentine peninsula, and wherever he went incognito, he was so loaded with unlooked for favours that he was puzzled by the contrast on his return to Naples. He could not fail to notice the coldness of Neapolitan society. But nobody is a prophet in his own country, he reflected.

His elder brother Hercules returned from his travels in ignorance of this state of affairs. In addition to being a skilled rider, a graceful dancer, a daring swordsman and a brilliant shot, he was far more prepossessing than his younger brother. He was the life and soul of any company, and brought home hearts by dozens, but he was also hot-headed and easily carried away. His mastery of weapons enabled him to kill or wound his adversary in any duel without ever a scratch to himself. Naturally, his self-assurance was increased by the respect his prowess inspired. Nobody in Naples was so rash as to challenge him. Soon after his return, a couplet was circulated which summarized the distinction between the two brothers:

> *"Challenged by Hercules, you're bound to die;*
> *But Isidore kills you calmly with his eye."*

Hercules still imagined that the whole of the family fortune was settled upon him, and it came as a shock to discover that the law of primogeniture had been repealed.

The reunion of the brothers was somewhat frigid, for they had scarcely met before and had no tender memories in common. While Hercules bore no grudge against Isidore for the sudden curtailment of his income, he was not sufficiently philosophical to forget it absolutely. But he was relieved to find that Isidore was no saintly simpleton, such as might have been expected from his monastic education. The candid hero-worship of this younger brother who had been brought up in quarantine, as it were, touched his simple, sturdy nature. And Isidore delighted in the society of Hercules, who had assumed a tone of good fellowship he had never experienced from another human being.

Hercules was the first person who had condescended to talk to him frankly as man to man, and they soon elicited mutual sympathies. Many balls and festivities were given in his honour, and though Isidore was never invited he showed no sign of resentment. There was only one fly in the ointment. Hercules could not understand why, with all his affability, Isidore seemed to have no friends. He took him to fashionable routs and assemblies, and while Hercules was invariably surrounded by a welcoming throng, Isidore was left in the lurch, pathetic and lonely. Whatever circle Isidore approached was apt to break up: the members drifted away.

Hercules could not fail to notice this, and it irked him. After the Countess of Mirafiore had swooned in the middle of a sentence which Isidore's sudden arrival interrupted, Hercules had resolved to tackle him on the subject. It looked as if he had been involved in a nasty scandal, and it must have been serious for the easy-going Neapolitans to behave in such a manner.

But Hercules could detect no clue. Isidore retained an air of child-like innocence.

"I was infatuated with the Countess," he admitted. "Perhaps I was a trifle hasty in declaring my passion, but she had received me with all the outward distinction accorded usually to a lover. All evening she had never left my arm, and when she proposed adjourning to her boudoir, I naturally tried to take advantage of it. Wouldn't you have done the same?"

Hercules laughed heartily. "Perhaps you went too far?"

"Would to Heaven I had gone farther! But I was a novice in such matters. It was not long since I had left the seminary. After taking me to her sanctum she contrived to topple over, revealing far more than her petticoats, I assure you. Then she galloped off to her bedroom, but I was too dazed to follow her at once. I think she was hoping to be ravished, and suddenly changed her mind. At any rate when I called again the door was slammed in my face."

"Evidently her conscience was ill at ease, though she diddles her *cavalier servente* with all the French officers. She will have to pay for it when the King returns to Naples. On the whole it was lucky that you restrained yourself. Have you made enemies on her account?"

39

"None that I am aware of. Several might have been jealous of the favour she showed me at her reception, but that was never repeated." Isidore heaved a sigh.

After bantering him on this episode, Hercules volunteered some sound advice. "This inordinate regard for a woman," said he, "must be abandoned. The chuck-under-the-chin, kindly-making-much-of, half-in-earnest and wholly patronizing air is the thing after all. Give exalted sentiment to nature and religion, and only familiar and casual affection to woman. But perhaps you have compromised yourself by meddling in politics? I sincerely hope not. It is no business for a gentleman. Under present conditions we must be polite to the French, but we need not exaggerate like the Mirafiore. Our good King Nosey will outlast Napoleon."

"The only Frenchmen I have met were at the Mirafiore's house. She leads the new craze for liberty."

"Liberty, what crimes are committed in thy name! Consider the extortion which the liberty-loving French have practised on us poor Italians, the high-flown lies, the statues and pictures pillaged! Whether under the French, the Austrians or the Spaniards, we suffer the same ill-treatment. Our Bourbons, with all their faults, are less hypocritical. Let us patiently await their return."

Isidore agreed with these sentiments. He would have agreed with anyone who was kind.

Thus Hercules came no nearer to solving the mystery. Was Isidore a dark horse after all? If not, why was society so prejudiced against him?

Hercules had not returned a fortnight without overhearing snatches of conversation which put him on his guard. His ears began to tingle when Isidore was mentioned, and eventually he nailed the rumour down.

A wag was entertaining a group of gossips with the saga of Isidore's feats of *jettatura*. He made horns with his fingers and rolled his eyes in mock terror each time he pronounced the unmentionable name. While he was describing the Countess's sensational party, Hercules joined his audience unperceived.

"Sometimes," said the wag, "the Evil Eye appears in one shape, sometimes in another, but it has never assumed so dangerous a shape before. It is a wonder that he does not blast himself with his own reflection, as in the old Greek poem:

'Fair was Eutelidas once, with his beautiful hair,
But admiring his face in a pool, on himself he inflicted
A dread fascination, and wasted away with disease.'

Be wise in time, my dears! Forewarned is forearmed. That perambulating catastrophe"—he made several signs of the Cross—"was the death of his mother at birth. He'll be the death of us all unless we take pains to prevent it. I tremble for his brother Hercules. The poor devil's bound to come a cropper before long."

"Hell and damnation, you lie!" Prince Hercules hurled a glove at the speaker's mouth.

Such a challenge could only be met with sword or pistols, and the rash entertainer had cause to tremble indeed. The glove had stung him like a whip, leaving a crimson mark on his livid cheek. Seconds were chosen from among the witnesses, and the duel was arranged for the next day.

Had good King Nosey been in Naples the police would have taken measures to stop it, but under the Republic this would have been considered a gross interference with personal liberty. Isidore got wind of it from one of his grooms, but the details were vague. Much perturbed, he asked Hercules if there was any truth in the rumour.

After beating about the bush, Hercules had to acknowledge that there was. But since, he added, a lady's honour was involved, he could let nobody into the secret, not even his own brother. Isidore appreciated this scrupulous delicacy, but he begged Hercules to let him act as his second. At first Hercules demurred, but Isidore was so insistent that he finally consented, on condition that he made no further inquiries or attempted any alternative settlement, however humiliating to his adversary.

Hercules left the choice of arms to his opponent, and they were to meet at six o'clock next morning by the shore of Lake Agnano. The crestfallen wag chose sabres. Hercules was equally at home with every type of weapon, but he had an emphatic preference for sabres, so he was in high spirits that night. The old Prince, his father, was still living in retirement at his ancestral castle and heard nothing of this affair.

Isidore drank more wine than usual in toasting his brother's victory, and Hercules held forth about his previous duels and the women who had provoked them.

In London a noble peer had divorced his wife after

catching her "in flagrant delight" with him. When on the point of marrying her, Hercules discovered that he had a competitor in her coachman. "I was rudely disillusioned," he said, "but she taught me a useful lesson. She was a placid blonde, of almost spiritual beauty. Her hazel eyes seemed the very mirrors of virtue. Till then I had always associated with blondes the idea of domestic bliss. Henceforth I turned to dark-eyed women—to the raven tresses and warm vivacity of brunettes. This bias was put to a severe test in France, but it has been confirmed in Italy."

In Paris and Vienna he had had so many adventures that he had not related half of them when Isidore suggested that they should retire for a few hours' rest.

Isidore could not sleep a wink: he turned and tossed in an agony of suspense about the next day's duel. But Hercules slept so soundly that Isidore had much ado to wake him. Though he shook him vigorously and twirled the bedclothes off, cold water had to be applied before he roused himself.

"You had better stay here and let me take your place," said Isidore. "You are far too drowsy to parry a blow from a sabre."

Hercules leapt out of bed. "I had forgotten," he exclaimed. "Please pour me a cup of chocolate."

He was soon dressed, and they set out in a coach, accompanied by a surgeon, as prescribed in the regulations. Isidore was dreadfully shaky, but his brother was hilarious, waving to every winsome wench they passed on the way.

The others appeared on horseback at the entrance to

the grotto of Pozzuoli. The four young men exchanged greetings and withdrew into the womb of the grotto. Ten minutes later they were standing on the shore of Lake Agnano.

Both parties had brought their own weapons and they threw dice to decide which were to be used. The dice favoured Hercules, and the disparity between the opponents was obvious. Isidore's detractor had had no experience of sabres, which he had chosen from desperate bravado, while Hercules handled his with a masterful poise and precision. Yet they had scarcely drawn before Hercules was pierced through the body. He fell without uttering a cry. The surgeon ran towards him, only to ascertain that the sabre had penetrated his heart.

Wild with grief, Isidore's first impulse was to avenge his brother. He seized Hercules's sabre and challenged the bloody murderer to settle accounts with him. But the surgeon and the other second intervened, declaring that this was against the rules of duelling.

In the meantime, the victor had fainted at the sight of blood. When he came to, he flung himself weeping upon the body of Hercules. Isidore indignantly attempted to remove him, but he was raving and tearing his hair, and it became evident that he had lost his wits. "You are to blame for this," he shouted at Isidore. "You are the real murderer of your brother—your Evil Eye!"

Isidore grappled with him and there was a furious wrestling match beside the corpse, in the midst of which his demented antagonist knelt down and wailed: "May God in Heaven forgive me!"

44

"Only Satan in Hell will forgive you," said Isidore, who was led home in a state of collapse.

The shock of this news proved mortal to Prince Pizzofalcone, who had anchored his last hopes in Hercules. When he was told that Isidore was awaiting outside, a look of horror came into his face and he uttered unintelligible sounds. He refused to see his only surviving son.

"Away with the fiend!" he cried, and his weak voice grew shrill and piercing. "He has brought enough misery into my life. He has killed both his mother and brother; he will now kill me."

His valet helped him to bed, and sent for the chaplain. But in his throat the ominous rattling had begun, and before the chaplain had time to administer extreme unction, the Prince was dead.

Thus at the age of twenty-one Isidore was left in sole possession of the Pizzofalcone fortune, one of the greatest in the Two Sicilies.

ISIDORE shut himself up in the palace and gave full vent to his grief, wandering about the darkened rooms like a man out of his mind.

His brother had been his first and only friend. By losing him he felt he had lost everything. Of what use was all his wealth, when he had nobody to help him enjoy it? Life itself had become unbearable to him. He sank into despondent brooding, which was exacerbated by his isolation.

He had never really known his father. The old Prince had been like a callous deity, influencing his life from afar. Isidore had always hoped to know him, if only to discover the reason for his inhumanity. There must be a reason: perhaps he was not his true begetter. . . .

What had he done to deserve such harsh treatment? Surely he had a right to be told? But the Prince had died with his secret.

"I never asked to be born," he reflected. "It was not my will to be plunged into this cauldron. I had no chance to choose my character, form or features. I could only make the best of circumstances beyond my control."

He had tried sincerely to fulfil his duties to God and man, and now he felt he was being punished, as if for a crime. "My crime is in being alive. I should have died at birth."

But Providence must have a motive and Isidore was still curious enough to investigate this, since that materialization of Providence, his father, had left no explanation. Though he came near to blowing his brains out, it was this intellectual curiosity which saved him.

His education had not prepared him for his present position. His prodigious wealth, his exalted rank, could not prevent him from feeling stranded. But he was a Christian believer, and when he tried to express the dim desperation of his thoughts to his aged confessor, that worthy man assured him that he had been placed on this earth for a divine purpose. It was not for him to question that purpose, but to accept it. "The French are demolishing man's faith," he told him. "Another crusade should be launched to defend and restore it. Your status, supported by money, gives you power. It is your plain duty to use it for the saving of souls."

"What about saving my own? It is in a deplorable plight. I am tormented by hideous nightmares and gloomy presentiments. Why did my father refuse to see me on his deathbed? I must be accursed," he cried, "accursed!"

"Do not blaspheme, my child," said his confessor. "Do not show such base ingratitude to your heavenly Maker! You are abundantly blessed with the goods of this world, and it depends on you whether you will be blessed with the goods of the next."

"Do you call it blessed to lose my nearest and dearest?"

"Your sorrow does you credit as a human being. It is a sweet incense soaring to those in Heaven. But it would be sinful to let it master you. There are others to live for, beginning with our Lord, who was crucified for your sake. The Lord has given, the Lord has taken away; blessed be the name of the Lord. The Lord has given far more to you than to most of us here below. Accept these manifest mercies and be grateful. Beg pardon for your sins and go on your way rejoicing."

These words brought Isidore a grain of comfort. His thoughts ceased to dwell on that past which he could not understand. As to the future—he had come, as it were, to a parting of the ways. He must trust in the powers that guided him. These powers infused fresh energy into him when he roamed the country on horseback.

The thoroughbreds that Hercules had brought from England were all so unruly that Isidore could only mount them with the utmost difficulty. He tried one after another, and as soon as he sprang into the saddle the horse set off at a crazy canter, as if startled by lightning. After cantering for miles, the beast became submissive. Each time he rode he experienced the same struggle: the horse kicked and plunged, tossed its head and foamed at the mouth. And each time he had to select a different horse, since it invariably returned to the stable broken-winded. Galloping hell for leather, Isidore grew calm. The animal's agitation relieved his own.

At length the crisis in his soul was overcome. "I am now well launched on the waves of life," he told himself. The image pleased him, as if it were original. It persisted, moreover, as most rhetoric does not. Why roam the neighbourhood of Naples merely; why not the world? His physician had prescribed travel. Suddenly it coincided with his mood. Talking of being launched, and of waves, he had never been to sea. If he had been put on earth for a divine purpose, was the ocean included as well? He decided to tempt Fate further. Why not embark on a sea voyage now that France and England were at war?

The blue waters of the bay seemed to beckon to him. A thirty-gun French frigate was riding at anchor, its tricolour waving to him from the mast-head. Hearing that it was due to sail for Toulon, Isidore secured an introduction to the Captain, whose name was Lubin. The Frenchman thought Isidore suspiciously bizarre, but promised him a passage on being offered an exorbitant sum for it. "Are you a good sailor?" he inquired.

"I've never sailed in my life," said Isidore.

"The *Incroyable* is definitely a man of war. I must warn you that we have no luxuries on board."

"All the better," said Isidore. "I'm ready for whatever may happen, battles, hurricanes, shipwreck—ready even to be blown to perdition with the whole damned cargo."

"That's the spirit," said the Captain; "but I trust we'll have a safe and easy voyage."

"I'm prepared for the worst," said Isidore; "nay, I shall welcome it. You behold a desperate man."

An odd speech, thought the Captain, but Italians were prone to bombast. The sea would soon toss that nonsense out of him. He was bound to be seasick if he had not sailed before.

Captain Lubin chuckled, for his frigate was a boisterous bird. "I advise you to bring a supply of lemons in case it gets rough," said he, shaking Isidore's hand.

On telling some cronies about this queer customer, Captain Lubin was cautioned about his reputation. "You had better return the passage money," said one. "It is asking for trouble to have such an incubus on board. He was right to say he is desperate. He has every cause to be. I hope you're provided with horns. His glance is homicidal."

But Captain Lubin was one of those bluff sea-wolves who believed neither in God nor Mammon. "Why, he looks as if he would hardly say boo to a goose!" was his only comment.

All the portents pointed to a perfect voyage. The weather was ideal; the British fleet under Foote was cruising near Corfu; and Nelson was lolling with Emma Hamilton at Palermo.

As soon as Isidore boarded the *Incroyable* he felt a new man. Ere it had lifted anchor, he had lifted his, ridding himself of his hypochondriac familiar. When Naples was left behind, he saw his old self receding in the distance, or so he fancied. A holiday mood set in. He was exhilarated like a spring long pent-up, bubbling at the moment of release into a cheerful valley, a region where he was utterly unknown. He was exalted by the sight of the ocean, "yielding homage only to eternal laws," and the ultramarine horizon awakened in him the most lofty sentiments. He spent hours of romantic musings on the quarter-deck. Thus he assumed he was sailing out to meet the sirens, whose song he hoped to hear. He would never stop his ears with wax, not he!—or be bound to the mast of the ship. He longed, in his innocence, to be allured.

The *Incroyable* sailed with a fair wind and a flowing sheet for the first two days and nights. Isidore did not seem to notice that she rocked considerably. He paced the deck with a true sailor's footing. From time to time he took a cake of chocolate out of his pocket and munched a morsel with relish. At night he slept like a log.

Early on the third morning, while Isidore was beginning to think the sea monotonous, the Captain was roused by a call from the watch: "A mast to starboard!"

Captain Lubin seized his telescope and studied the sail in sight. He recognized a frigate of forty guns more powerful than his own. From its heavier build and other idiosyncrasies, he concluded it must be British. But ten guns more or less did not worry so seasoned a salt. He ordered his crew to prepare for action and continued to scrutinize the distant vessel, which was steering towards him. The Captain enjoyed what he called a game of bowls and felt quite equal to any emergency.

Then the watch called out again: "A mast to larboard!" Turning his telescope, Captain Lubin spied a second ship, its black profile approaching imperceptibly. He examined it with decreasing enthusiasm, for it was plainly a ship of the line. "It looks as if we're caught between two vicious fangs," he growled. He gave orders to steer for Bastia with all the sail the frigate could carry. The head-sails were clewed up in a twinkling, the rigging was sheepshanked and set up taut and the fore-topsail double reefed. The *Incroyable* ran before the wind with renewed vigour, as light as a seagull.

Isidore stood on the quarter-deck as a privileged spectator. He was conscious again of a change in himself. His excitement at sea was much less oppressive than the gloom which had invaded him on land. It was mingled with eager expectation of danger and a sense of heroism which was quite delicious.

On spotting the two hostile ships, he realized that the frigate's best chance was in rapid flight. Happily, the wind was favourable. The *Incroyable* had only to follow a straight course, while her two foes had to follow a diagonal. At her actual speed she would soon outsail the latter.

Captain Lubin, who had been busy shouting commands, began to relax and whistle the *Marseillaise*. Isidore strode up to him rubbing his hands. "Well, Captain, have we better legs than they?" he asked jovially.

"By blue, yes, and if this wind keeps blowing we'll leave them so far behind that their bark will be out of hearing."

Isidore earnestly fixed his gaze to windward. "Oh, the wind isn't likely to change," he said complacently. "Not if I know it."

"Ahoy, Captain!" bawled the boatswain.

"What's up now? Another crocodile?"

"The wind shifts from east to north."

"A thousand thunders, impossible!"

A northerly gust confirmed this deplorable news. It was so sudden that it was still open to query. The Captain waited a few minutes before clinching a decision, but soon there could be no doubt that a steady gale was blowing from the north. This would enable the warship to cut the road to Corsica. The enemy frigate was beginning to lose distance.

The Captain resolved to tackle the lighter ship before the heavier one hove to her assistance. He gave orders accordingly; the hammocks were stowed away, the artillery pointed, the musketry prepared, the axes and grapplings laid out, the cartridge and bullet stores made available, and the powder-room opened. All the hawsers and spare cables for strengthening the masts in case of need were heaped near the tiller-ropes by the gangway, and the cockpit was put in order for the wounded. When the drum was beaten for combat every man was at his post.

The *Incroyable* came within such close range of the British frigate that the latter's drum could be heard in answer to the challenge. Aware of her intention, the warship spread all its sails and made directly for her. The three vessels were soon in line: the *Incroyable* in the centre, was about a quarter league from the enemy frigate and about two leagues from the warship. When an engagement grew imminent, Captain Lubin asked Isidore to retire below. But Isidore was longing to be "baptized by fire," and he begged leave to remain on deck. The Captain, who liked pluck, consented.

They had barely advanced a hundred feet when a puff of cloud appeared on the British frigate. This was followed by an explosion on the *Incroyable*, and a filmy vapour which vanished through the rigging, as if driven by the wind from France. The two frigates drew closer, and though the French guns were itching to reply, no other sound could be

54

heard but the *Marseillaise*, which the Captain continued to whistle. Perhaps it was the only tune he knew, for he adapted it to every occasion and its message varied with the Captain's mood. Just now it sounded aggressive, as if it had a sting in its tail.

The silent ship, sweeping towards the foe in a straight line with wings as firm as an eagle's, was a gallant sight. Finally, the two frigates were almost alongside each other.

After discharging her first volley without any damage to the *Incroyable*, the British vessel veered round and exposed her best-armed flank to the French artillery. The order to fire was answered by thirty guns simultaneously. One third of the British crew were annihilated; the top-mast, main-mast and mizzen-mast were shot to pieces; and shuddering from stem to stern, the British vessel stopped as if hypnotized.

The *Incroyable* saluted with her second volley, and soon there was the shock of both vessels colliding and grappling irons tangling in an embrace which must prove deadly to one or the other. A pandemonium followed, with Englishmen and Frenchmen in such confusion that it was not clear who was attacking and who defending.

Thrice the French leapt forward in a torrent to board the British vessel, and thrice they were repulsed. On the fourth attempt all resistance appeared to cease. The British Captain had either been killed or wounded. When the French sailors were clambering on the enemy decks, the British Captain appeared with a firebrand from the hold: he had done quick work and his ship was soon ablaze. All hands rushed pell-mell on to the *Incroyable* to escape the volcano yawning beneath them.

Captain Lubin barely managed to manœuvre his ship a little astern before the British frigate blew up with a frightful explosion, since she had a great quantity of gunpowder on board as well as other combustibles. Everything flew upwards, with such a field of red flame as illuminated the whole elements in broad daylight. A ghastly silence followed, and for a while a glowing oven of fiery timbers floated on the surface of the sea and burned to the water's edge, sinking gradually into a whirlpool of boiling waves.

Both ships had been so close that the *Incroyable* might also have been dragged to the ocean bottom or shot into the sky. Nobody could yet feel sure of his safety, and the bravest peered at each other in dismay.

Captain Lubin and Isidore were the first to recover their composure. One shell from the enemy had struck the sheet anchor and a piece of it fell near Isidore. He decided to keep it as a souvenir. The Captain ordered the few prisoners to be taken below and the dead to be thrown overboard. Corpses and parts of bodies, wrapped in tarpaulin, were slid down planks into the waves.

The enemy warship had made disconcerting progress during the interval.

The French frigate's masts and rigging were much cut up; her sails were ribbons and all her ropes were ends. The presence of danger inspired the old Captain with extraordinary vigour and he grew red as a

turkey-cock, rapping out rapid orders. All hands were employed to repair the rigging and bend a new set of sails as speedily as possible. Since survival depended on dispatch, they crowded all the sail the *Incroyable* could carry to cut off the foe, and several guns and spars were thrown overboard. Helm up she ran before the wind, but for all her lightness and speed, the enemy was drawing nearer, and when the latter was about to catch up with her manœuvres, the *Incroyable* downed steering sails and hauled on a wind again.

As she seemed on the verge of escaping, a shell pierced the main top-mast and cut several cables. "A thousand thunders!" growled the Captain. "The pirates have twenty-four-pounders."

Two guns of this calibre were in fact fixed fore and

aft of the enemy man-of-war, so that when Captain Lubin fancied himself out of range he was well under enemy fire. "Out with all the canvas, every inch of it. Use even your pocket handkerchiefs if need be."

Four petty sails were run up to support the others, and there was a noticeable increase of speed, but this was not sufficient. Again the warship opened fire with her guns, but all her shot went overhead and nobody was injured.

For some time the Captain's eye remained glued to his telescope, then he smacked it against his palm with an air of relief. "You have lost the race, you bloodhounds. We're half a knot faster than you."

"Shall we be clear of them by to-morrow?" asked Isidore, who had never left the deck.

"If we keep up this speed," replied the Captain.

"And if no wicked cannon ball breaks one of our legs," added Isidore with a chuckle.

Just then a ball snapped the mast against which Isidore was standing. It toppled over the deck, burying him under a mound of cordage and canvas.

A violent oath was the Captain's only comment. His situation had become critical. Another action was inevitable. With an inferior ship, men weary from the previous engagement, and a crew but half as numerous as the foe, the dice were loaded heavily against him. But to face ill fortune with a bold front is the custom of those who rule at sea. Hammocks were piped up, the guns got ready, and the drums beat lustily to quarters. The decks were cleared; superfluous sails and rigging were cast into the waves. It was only then that Isidore was discovered, safe and sound.

The enemy had made a considerable advance. Escape was contemptible when it offered scant chance of survival; at least the Captain thought so. To encourage his men, he called them aft on the quarterdeck and delivered a curt speech: "Friends, all of us are sunk from A to Z. If we must die, we must—it's all in the day's work. One resource remains to us: it is better to fight to our last breath like sailors. Hurrah for the Republic!"

The crew cheered and ran to their stations as to a distribution of rum. Captain Lubin stood as cool as a cucumber, while the shot dropped about him like hail. One bounced on the forecastle and took the boatswain's head off; another hit her near the water's edge; only a few went over the frigate. When the enemy was within close range it wrapped itself in a mantle of smoke and raked the frigate's decks. Captain Lubin gave orders to run alongside the foe and try to board her.

The foe blazed away with great vigour, manœuvring so as to keep the *Incroyable* at the same distance. Each broadside struck the frigate full amidships; her own fire was lost in the limbo separating her from the target. It was a death rattle rather than a battle.

Captain Lubin stood in the most exposed positions in the hope that a cannon ball would finish him off. But he seemed as invulnerable as Isidore, who had followed all the proceedings with the same impassive mien. While the *Incroyable* was raked from stem to stern and the main deck was littered with corpses and mangled limbs, he went unscathed. Seeing his crew decimated without hope of reprisal while the ship shuddered and groaned beneath him, he felt acutely responsible. Crying with rage, he gave orders to lower the standard.

Enemy fire ceased as soon as the tricolour was hauled down. The British warship hove towards the *Incroyable*, who watched her approach in grim silence. Even the dying stopped their groans. Instinctively the survivors manned the remaining guns, but at a signal from the Captain the batteries were dismantled.

The two ships were abreast of each other, but in vastly different plight. Not one of the British crew was missing and all the warship's masts and sails were intact, whereas the *Incroyable* was dismasted and unmanageable, with most of her port lids shot away and guns dismounted. Part of her hull was broken, and this

had to be patched up with tarpaulin and plank so as to keep her afloat. Her torn rigging flapped in the wind like a lunatic's hair.

When the British Captain was within vocal range, he addressed his valiant adversary through his speaking-trumpet in fluent French, telling him he was a brave fellow for defending his ship so well. Captain Lubin shrugged his shoulders and signalled for a tender, since his own was *hors de combat*. First the serious casualties were moved, then those with minor wounds, and finally the few who had escaped sound in wind and limb with Isidore.

Captain Lubin remained on board till the very last. When all his crew had left the ship and the British commander was sending his own gig for him, he retired to his cabin as if he had forgotten something. A few minutes later a pistol shot was heard. Two British tars and a midshipman ran to the Captain's cabin. They found him weltering in a pool of blood. Unwilling to survive defeat, he had shot himself through the head.

The two tars and the midshipman had barely ascertained his death when they heard a piercing whistle. As soon as Isidore had boarded the victorious warship the weather began to change. The wind had swung round, the sea was rising, and a squall, perhaps a tempest, threatened. Since there was no time to lose, the Captain decided to bear up for the nearest port. As the gale was gathering strength, he could not carry an inch of sail, but was compelled to let the ship drive as the wind and waves drove her; he got his top-gallant masts down on deck and made everything as secure as possible. Soon the wind began to blow great guns. The sky grew dark as pitch with the sea running mountains high.

Her mainmast cut away, the ship was scudding under bare poles. The heavy battery of waves stove in the bulwark on the weather side of the forecastle, sprang the bowsprit, carried off the mainstay and drew some of the main rigging channel-bolts out. Another blow unshipped her rudder. All the pumps were set to work, and the roaring wind and waves drove her along, until the want of a rudder caused her to sheer to port and enter the harbour of Toulon, lashed by the final blast of the storm which had all but sunk her. Peace between France and Britain had recently been patched up at Amiens, so the crew were permitted to land with their Italian passenger.

After various formalities, Isidore thanked the Captain for his hospitality and bade him farewell. "I wish you the fairest of winds on your return journey," he said heartily. But the dilapidation of the vessel was irreparable, and despite all efforts to make her seaworthy, she ran against a rock with such force that she stove in her larboard side and went to the bottom.

On disembarking at Toulon, Isidore found a comfortable inn and slept solidly for twenty-four hours.

ISIDORE had been more exhausted than he realized. When he awoke he shuddered agreeably at the recollection of all the dangers he had escaped. They had given his mind a beneficial shock. "We are all propelled by forces we imperfectly comprehend, but I was right to embark on that voyage," he decided.

Until then he had been utterly in the mist about himself. Now the darkness was partially lifted. Danger had proved an antidote to his distress. He had not heard the song of the sirens, but he had seen the forces of nature in commotion, and in those fractions of time when he had been nearest to death he had become more aware of living. The particular had been revealed in the universal; and he was confident that he was part of the divine. He was still uncertain of his goal, but he was endowed with a new strength and stability to guide him towards it.

The little maid who brought him his chocolate was bewitchingly pretty. About fifteen, he presumed, though her bosoms were so ripe that they were ready to pop through her bodice. Their tips pointed provocatively in his direction. And her eyes—what an inviting sparkle! He could not resist giving her a chuck under the chin. Before he knew it she had fallen into his arms.

He had never tasted anything so succulent as her lips, which slipped in and out of his own like a couple of cool wet cherries. Her lithe arms encircled his neck, and he lost no time in carrying her where she belonged.

This is absurd, he chuckled inwardly; I am no sooner out of bed than I return to it—but in what delicious company!

The next twenty-four hours were thus spent in the same situation, but in different circumstances. His partner was as inexhaustible as himself in the pursuit of amorous pleasure. Her little tongue found its way everywhere; so did his. And her little teeth woke him up when he began to drowse and spurred him on to fiercer flights of discovery. This was wonderful exercise after the cramping austerities of life on board ship. His very soul expanded by leaps and bounds. The bed was transformed into another ship of war, heaving in another ocean, with the sheets flying like sails in the gust of his passion. The pillows became billows.

Isidore was captain of this vessel, and it performed prodigious manœuvres under his command. The storm had entered his chamber like a whirlwind, and he clung to his melting mate with all his sinews, as to some miraculous rudder, straining them to the utmost.

"*Doucement, chéri*, more gently! You're hurting me," she gasped.

He relaxed his grip and gazed into her eyes. Tears glistened on the lashes. He licked them off, and their salty flavour renewed his thirst for her lips. Off again, he altered his course, ploughing the ocean more steadily and surely, panting with rapture the while.

"We're at sea," he explained, "but I'll steer you safely to port."

Lisette, for such was her name, felt rather frightened. This was a very tempestuous gentleman! What extraordinary eyes. Perhaps he was a little mad. But then, she reflected, 'tis I that made him so.

She had the presence of mind to say, "Steer me to Paris. I have never been to Paris."

"To Paris, ahoy!" he shouted. "We'll set all the sail we can carry and run before the wind."

He was making such a din that the landlord knocked at the door. "This is really going too far," he grumbled to his wife. "I have no objection to Lisette's disappearance. On the contrary, it means more money. She'll hand me a percentage of her earnings and I'll get a fat gratuity from the customer. If he's rich I can even pretend that she is my daughter and try on a bit of blackmail. But all this creaking and pounding and shouting—it will give my house a bad name. People will wonder what is going on here. I'm wondering myself. It has been going on for hours. Bang, bang, bang—it's high time I put a stop to it."

"Hi, you two," he shouted through the keyhole. "I'm not asking indiscreet questions, but for Heaven's sake keep quiet. After a hard day's work there are folks who need some rest. *Ne soyez pas égoistes.*"

"Beat to quarters and get the guns ready," shouted Isidore. "Now open fire! That's right, blaze away! The enemy's sinking. They're totally dismasted. Hurrah, they're sunk. *Vive la République!*"

"Are you mad in there?" asked the landlord.

For all answer the bed creaked and heaved, the mattresses bounced up and down, and there was a sound of tussling, interspersed with gluttonous gurglings and frolicsome shrieks.

"*Dis donc, Lisette, sois sage!* Don't exaggerate. This is not the time or place for wrestling matches."

"You're sunk," said Isidore, hurling a chamber-pot at the door.

"That settles it," shouted the landlord. "I'll call the gendarmes." Of course he had no such intention. He could tell a rich man when he saw one, and he was charging Isidore double for his room.

After a peal of giggles from Lisette, the noise died down. The young couple nestled together like turtle-doves in a state of sweet fatigue. So much exercise had prepared both of them for sleep, and they slept without dreams, impervious to the crowing of cocks and the bustle in the courtyard.

Isidore was the first to waken, and he rubbed his eyes in amazement at the bosoms swelling beside him. He contemplated the indolent form in ecstasy. Soft curves of the smoothest ivory, long rippling curls in rain adown the pillow, and parted lips still moist, as if flecked with dew.

Lisette was more marvellous than he had imagined; she was also far more mature. During the night she seemed to have increased in girth as well as stature. Surely her breasts had been smaller yesterday? They had expanded into rounder roses, none the less beautiful for being less firm. Her hips were more massive; and the long legs were sprinkled with a fine down he had not noticed before. Even her chin was plumper, with two new dimples.

Am I growing near-sighted, he wondered, or have my caresses wrought this miracle? I slept with a nymph and waken to find a Juno. She is certainly nearer thirty than thirteen. All in a night she has attained to sublime proportions.

If anything, she had seemed a trifle too slim at first. Now she could not be too substantial for Isidore's appetite. An intense pallor had taken the place of the vivid colours which had animated her under the lamp-light. She reclined superb amid the havoc of soiled and crumpled sheets, like a waxen figure sculptured by Canova. Isidore leaned over her quivering with emotion, admiring the contrast between her satin and his shagginess.

Lisette had opened to him a world of happiness, and the sunlight streaming upon her intensified her beauty and his wonder. Her blue-lidded eyes were closed. He brushed them lightly with his lips. The lashes flickered, and the sleepy pools bestirred themselves and watched him in vague alarm.

"Why, you're bigger than I thought," she exclaimed.

"So are you," he retorted laughing.

As he kissed her she wailed: "You're scratching me. Mercy, what a beard you have grown! You're covered with stiff prickles. Please wait until you have shaved."

"I can't wait another minute," said he, and gripped her in his arms like a pair of vices.

Her terror rendered her even more alluring. "You're crushing me to death," she gasped. "Help, help!"

Lisette's cries and the renewed racket brought the landlord up again. His batterings on the door increased the pounding of Isidore's heart and added fresh fuel to his ardour. After a while, when Lisette slipped away from him in a stupor, Isidore donned a brocaded dressing-gown and flung open the door.

"How dare you interrupt my diversions?" he drawled in his grandest manner. "Go immediately and fetch me a ham, four beefsteaks rare, a bowl of mixed salad, a selection of cheese and fruit, and two bottles of the best champagne, or by Heaven I'll blow your brains out!"

Catching sight of a brace of pistols on the table, the landlord was off in a twinkling. "Our Lisette has done well for herself," he told his wife. "She has hooked a distinguished foreigner of extravagant tastes."

"I don't trust those foreigners," said his wife. "And I'll give Lisette the scolding she deserves for raising such a rumpus. *Ce n'est pas convenable.* I couldn't sleep a wink all night."

"Neither could I," yawned the landlord, "but we're only young once, my cabbage." He gave her a smacking kiss and pinched her behind.

"What has come over you?" asked his wife, unused to such attentions. "Leave go. I've the steaks to prepare."

"They can wait. Let's run upstairs. We're only young once, you know."

"Are you crazy all of a sudden? There must be an epidemic in the house."

For answer he seized and carried her, still protesting, out of the kitchen.

"That breakfast is a long time coming," said Isidore. "I'm simply ravenous. Shall we raid the larder?"

"Leave everything to me," said Lisette, suddenly practical. "I'm an expert cook, and I'm feeling quite peckish myself."

"I can't bear you to leave my sight," said Isidore.

"Well, then, you come along and mix the salad."

They found the kitchen deserted, which was unusual at this hour of the day. What if the landlord had gone for the police, Lisette wondered. But Isidore assured her that he would do no such thing. "And even if he did, I enjoy diplomatic immunity as a foreign prince."

"A prince? Get along with you! There are no more princes since the revolution."

"In any case, he won't kill the goose that lays the golden eggs."

"You'd make a fine *pâté*. No need for forcible feeding!"

Isidore demolished half a ham while the steaks were sizzling. How prettily Lisette prodded them with her fork! Her bare arms gleamed all the whiter among the sooty pots and pans, and her face was flushed by the glow of the oven.

"I shall have an atrocious kitchen smell," she complained. "It gets into my hair."

"The best perfume in the world," sighed Isidore with a sniff.

"Only because you happen to be hungry. It isn't so nice when you have gorged your fill."

"I would always be hungry in your company," he replied, flinging more garlic into the salad bowl. "Just now you look like a cannibal queen, grilling the hearts of your victims."

"You're the cannibal. You certainly made a meal of me last night. I dare not show myself until those bites have healed."

"That suits me perfectly. I'm jealous. I don't want others to see you."

"I'm not your property," she pouted.

"Perhaps not; but I am yours."

This rejoinder brought her to the table smiling with

the beefsteaks. Her appetite whetted his as it was about to wane. All the same it was impossible to keep pace with him. He ate with ferocious rapidity. The big ham had all but collapsed: a few slivers remained with the bone.

"Not so quickly," cautioned Lisette as he was hoisting a chunk of steak into his mouth. "You'll burn your tongue."

"You've done that already," he said, devouring it like a tiger. "Where's the champagne? Let us open it."

The popping of corks made him boisterous. He dabbled his fingers in the foam from the two bottles and applied them first behind the rims of Lisette's ears, then behind his own.

Lisette was extremely light-headed, and a couple of glasses reduced her to hopeless giggles. Isidore had a whim to tickle her, and while she was wriggling away from him her bodice flew open. He stood flabbergasted at the sight. Was it possible for anyone to change so suddenly? Her bust was monumental. How could he have imagined her a giddy girl of fifteen?

At this moment the landlord and his spouse crept back into the kitchen. They too looked somewhat flustered and dishevelled.

"Still at it? Fie, for shame!" exclaimed the landlady. "Must you choose my respectable kitchen for your tousling and mousling? Button yourself in, you baggage. As for you, Mr. Satyr"—she turned towards Isidore with a rolling pin—"I advise you to settle your account and be packing, or I'll denounce you for debauching a virgin under age."

Isidore laughed in her face. "Under what age, madam? Take a good look at the girl and answer me that."

The landlord and his wife both gaped at Lisette and then at each other, dumfoundered and round-eyed. They gaped again and exclaimed: "Sure, it cannot be the same person. This wench is five, nay ten years older than our Lisette."

Despite Lisette's protestations, they refused to believe in her identity. This was clearly someone else. They apologized to Isidore profusely. Lisette must have given them the slip.

As a result of this misapprehension, Isidore had no difficulty in taking Lisette to Paris. He congratulated himself on having found so satisfactory a mistress and travelling companion. Before leaving Toulon he renewed her wardrobe, promising to renew it again when they reached Paris. The fantastic pace of her physical development would make this a necessity.

"I'm so happy, so happy," she kept repeating. "Tell me, do you find me altered?"

Isidore deemed it politic to answer in the negative.

"Don't be silly! Can't you see what has happened to me since we met?"

"I've made a woman of you."

"Don't flatter yourself, duckie."

"You're one year older."

"You must be going blind. I'm ages younger!"

Isidore wondered what she would say next. He was puzzled by the abrupt contrast between her words and her appearance. On the spur of the moment she

73

showed a double chin which he had not noticed before, and there was the shade of a mustachio on her upper lip.

"Yes, I'm years younger," she claimed; "and all because you made me fall in love with you. Pick me up and see how much lighter I am."

Isidore was fairly strong, but now with his utmost exertions he could not lift her from the ground. And only recently he had carried her to bed with the greatest of ease. But the mind is ever reluctant to consent to reality. How hard it was to trust the evidence of the senses! He tried to hoist her again and again with no better success. At last he dropped exhausted in a chair, mopping the sweat off his brow. Lisette did not realize the transformation. Should he enlighten her?

"You must be worn out with the pleasures of love, my angel. You had better take a long, long rest in a single bed."

This annoyed Isidore, and he set about proving the contrary there and then. After a while it was Lisette who complained of fatigue. Verily she seemed on the brink of middle age. New wrinkles appeared about her eyes and mouth, which was drooping at the corners.

On waking up in the morning he was so shocked by the multitudinous folds of fat heaving beside him that he could hardly steel himself to respond to her caresses. When her sagging lips groped for his in a semi-coma, he jumped out of bed. The ghastly thought flashed through him: what if he had grown equally old? Time had passed with delusive speed, and perhaps it had played him another scurvy trick. What if his

face were seamed with wrinkles and his hair had turned
snow-white? Was he shrinking? Had he grown thinner?
Lisette mocked all his notions of what was permissible.
He dare not consult the mirror. Instead, he peered
with repulsion at the form he had left in bed with
flabby arms outstretched towards him.

"Another kiss, just a little one," she whined in a
wizened voice. "Assure me that you will love me
always. I need consolation; I have a raging toothache."

What on earth was he to do with this amorous
elephant? He was too soft-hearted to send her back
to Toulon. His conscience reminded him that he had
begun this idyll. But she was growing older by leaps
and bounds, as if attacked by some galloping disease.
But age was incurable, he reflected. To wake up every
morning a little less young than the day before, to lose
one's hair and see it fade from grey to white, to feel
oneself wither slowly and suffer aches and pains
precisely when knowledge was beginning to intensify
enjoyment—it was cruelly unfair!

A ruin often had its own magnificence: he thought
of the Roman Colosseum—yet he would not have
enjoyed watching the progress of its decrepitude.
Still less did he fancy looking on at Lisette's deterioration. Her jaw was swollen, and there she was still
clamouring to be kissed!

"Get up and dress, dear," he said. "If we are to
reach Paris before nightfall it is time you put some
clothes on."

"You have changed," said Lisette. "You are no
longer the same sweet man."

So it was true! Isidore started to tremble. He made a dash for the looking glass.

"Yes, you no longer love me," she nagged on. "Yet I have given you my youth. I have sacrificed a woman's all."

Isidore laughed triumphantly at the reflection which met his gaze. He looked absurdly young, a mere boy.

"Admiring yourself, eh? Preening yourself like a peacock. What selfish brutes men are!"

He raised the lids of his eyes, patted his cheek approvingly, turned his head from right to left, and, after a graceful pirouette, bowed like a courtier before his own reflection.

In the meantime, Lisette had burst into tears, which did not enhance her beauty. Her clothes were already too tight for her, but with strenuous assistance from Isidore she was eventually corseted and covered. When he helped her into the coach, she leaned on him as if he were a crutch. He nearly toppled over. Apparently she was suffering from rheumatism as well as toothache.

She complained continuously of the jolting of the carriage. That she was amply padded with flesh seemed no protection. It was a clumsy contrivance, more like a stage-coach than a private vehicle, and its unsteadiness was due to the poor quality of the springs, which were fastened with ropes to make them more effective. Access to the interior was through a narrow door on a level with the wheels. Isidore had not been able to find a more comfortable conveyance. The public *diligence* was even more unsteady.

Though Isidore plied Lisette with draughts of brandy, her temper did not improve. She was the reverse of an agreeable companion, fretful and fussy except when her mouth was full, and then she dribbled. At frequent intervals she would stop the carriage to relieve nature. This delayed the journey considerably.

Everybody mistook Lisette for Isidore's mother. He kept a stiff upper lip, but he felt acutely embarrassed. How would this adventure end?

By the time they entered Paris not a vestige of the original Lisette remained. Instead of a vivacious wench, he found himself saddled with a decrepit dame. To make matters worse, she fancied herself sixteen. Her own mirror failed to enlighten her. She insisted on being taken everywhere, to the Opera, the Comedy, and all the haunts of frivolity and fashion.

Paris was then the most sensual city in the world, and the one in which pleasure was carried to its highest pitch, but, excepting the quays and a few of the bridges, Isidore could find little to appreciate after Naples. See Naples and die, he murmured.

The curiosity of the Parisians was proverbial, and when Isidore arrived with Lisette they were stared at as if they had dropped from the moon. Perhaps they would have stared less if he had been alone. Old men, young men, women and children were all pushing and scrambling to gape at his companion. As soon as Isidore took her out everybody rushed to the windows. In the Tuileries gardens and the Palais Royal they had a circle around them in no time, and he overheard such rude remarks as, "Make room for the hippopotamus."

Fortunately, Lisette was growing deaf. She imagined that they were crowding to admire her.

Her youthful energy revived as Isidore piloted her through the Faubourg St. Honoré: she wanted to cram herself with caramels at every confectionery and buy more millinery at every *modiste*. He could hardly drag her away from the shop windows. Still imagining herself sixteen, Lisette would leer and wink at passing strangers, and press Isidore's hand to her capacious bosom. He was too indignant to find these antics amusing. At the theatre she snored while opera glasses were levelled in her direction, but in the bed she insisted on sharing with him she remained awake till the small hours, reproaching him for his frigidity.

When he could bear it no longer he decided to break with her: he would be magnanimous and leave her with an old age pension. He was about to broach the subject when she announced that she was quick with child. "If you are a man of honour you will marry me," she added. "Now run and fetch me some strawberries. I have a mother's craving for them."

He fetched a doctor instead. The doctor felt her pulse and examined her tongue, then tapped his own forehead significantly.

"Tell me at once, is it to be a boy or a girl?" she croaked.

The doctor turned and whispered in Isidore's ear: "The delusions of extreme senility—a very sad case indeed. There is nothing much to be done, I'm afraid. You must try to humour her. In nine months' time she may forget about it. The imaginary pregnancy won't do her any harm."

"Can't you give her a soporific? She doesn't sleep at night."

"That was precisely what I was going to suggest. I'll prescribe a mild opiate. It is evident that her nervous system is out of order. At her advanced age she needs all the rest she can obtain, poor old lady. Such an excess of adipose tissue is deleterious to the heart. This delusion of hers is an ominous sign, but we must not let her suspect the truth. The shock of disappointment might prove fatal."

"Don't you hear me?" grumbled Lisette. "Are you deaf, Doctor? I asked if I was to expect a son or a daughter?"

"At this early stage it would be rash to predict," he replied.

"I do hope it is going to be a boy. There is no danger or risk, is there, Doctor? I'm even younger than I look, you know. Am I too much of a baby to have a baby?"

"Don't worry, Madame. At least I'm confident on that score," he replied urbanely. "She means she is in her second youth," he whispered to Isidore. "Give her the opiate now and let her sleep it off. Perhaps Paris has been too strenuous for her constitution."

The doctor proved right. Lisette had never slept more soundly. All attempts to wake her were vain.

When the doctor was summoned he shook his head. "The old lady's condition was more serious than I suspected," he pronounced. "I did not wish to alarm you yesterday, but the pulse was so languid that it was touch and go. To-day I can only offer my profound condolences."

A priest was sent for, and all arrangements were made for an expeditious funeral, to be followed by several Masses for the repose of her soul. Isidore presented a large sum to the poor of the parish in Lisette's memory, since he knew nothing about her next of kin. Owing to an intense heat wave, the burial could not be postponed.

Though Isidore tried to persuade himself that Lisette had only been a passing fancy, his thoughts kept returning to his first impression of her. It was as if their liaison had lasted for years and years. The experience left him contrite, but it never occurred to him that there was any link between this and his previous bereavements, though the combination of circumstances did strike him as singular.

ISIDORE decided to leave for England, since Lisette had spoiled the taste of France for him.

The Neapolitan envoy, who had received him after much procrastination and then somewhat distantly, grasping the coral horn on his watch-chain throughout their interview, became more effusive when he heard that Isidore was due to depart.

"So Your Highness is not returning to Naples?" he inquired.

"Eventually, of course," said Isidore, "but at the moment it is too full of tragic memories. My physician has prescribed a change of air. Misfortune has even pursued me to Paris, for I have lost a fond mistress within a week of my arrival. I hope for better luck in England. Now that peace is assured, I should like to take advantage of it."

"That finishes the peace," thought the ambassador, "it will end within less than a year. We shall see the war renewed with energy on both sides." He clutched his coral horn convulsively. "If there is anything I can do for you in the meantime, pray remember that I am entirely at your disposal," he stammered, avoiding Isidore's eye.

"As a stranger to Great Britain, I should be grateful for a few letters of recommendation."

"Your Highness shall have them before this evening. Thus provided, you will be assured of a hearty welcome among the fogs."

While escorting him to the staircase, the envoy slipped and sprained his ankle. At first he thought his leg was broken and yelled with the full force of his lungs. But his Neapolitan prudence soon got the upper hand. Injured as he was, he had the presence of mind to gasp: "Thanks! Your Highness might have killed me, and you have only sprained my ankle!"

Isidore concluded that he was being facetious. "Your Excellency is a humorist," he said. "Very droll, upon my word!"

"Thanks for sparing me. Thanks again! I shall not forget the letters of introduction, but pray do not trouble to call. I shall send them to your hotel."

The Neapolitan envoy in London was even more elusive than his colleague in Paris, and invented a thousand pretexts to keep Isidore at bay. But the English knew nothing of his legend; even had they been warned, they would have laughed at such outlandish superstition. Albeit a foreigner, as a young man of evident means and resounding title, he found many congenial houses open to him.

At first he devoted several hours a day to Shakespeare, but he found that conversing with his Cockney valet was more useful for practical purposes. He soon became master of an adequate vocabulary. A mere handful of words were current in society, and these always recurred with monosyllabic variations. With the aid of gesture, he was generally understood. His pronunciation afforded much simple mirth, and laughter paved the way to pleasant friendships. He was introduced to the Prince of Wales, who complimented him on the cut of his pantaloons and invited him to Brighton. He was baptized in ale at White's and driven to Newmarket. He danced endless quadrilles in the Ranelagh rotunda. And on all occasions he was lavish with his purse as with his person. No accident attended his appearances in public; at any rate, none was noticed. Ill luck was faint and weary with dogging his footsteps. Like Napoleon, it durst not cross the Channel.

Isidore was no longer spoken of with bated breath as the "*innominabile*" and the "*formidabile*." He was "the Vesuvian swell," "the amiable Prince Battledore and Shuttlecock," ever popular at routs and assemblies, a man's man and a lady's man to boot.

84

When he visited Bath there was keen rivalry among the damsels for his favour. As soon as the orchestra stopped playing in a ball-room his proficiency as a dancer was extolled, and all agreed that he had a consummate air of romance.

"He has the bold black eyes of a Barbary corsair," said one.

"But he's so gentle," said another. "His voice is soft and cooing like a dove's."

"It is rather too soft for a real man's. My husband maintains he is like those Italian singers of opera, whose conversation could never be dangerous to feminine virtue."

"I have often said that gentleness is power, and the violent are weaker than the mild."

"His morals may be lax, but not his posture. Observe that leg!"

"He smiles like a cupid, innocent and mischievous at the same time. . . ."

Their prattle became a competition of scissors in which each snips off the next remark that sprouts.

Isidore appeared unconscious of the sensation he produced. He showered his gifts impartially. This endeared him to the ladies all the more and kept them on tenterhooks. Some sent him letters proposing to leave husbands and children for his sake. A few parents had to remove their daughters to the country and clap them under lock and key when they discovered what follies they were perpetrating on his account, and several husbands were forced to be equally severe with their wives.

But the majority opined that he was a harmless sort of fellow, who was a favourite of the fair because he had renounced any compromising connection with them. The ladies found him ever ready to counsel, to cheer, to amuse, to befriend, to fulfil all kinds of delicate errands for them. Few Englishmen were so good-natured and obliging. To them female society was a pastime rather than a necessity; to Isidore it was both. Deprived of it, his mind lost healthful activity, his sentiment became morbid, his outlook dreary. But he had not forgotten his brother's misadventure with the English Countess, and he was determined to be cautious after his affair with Lisette.

One young lady blushed deeper than the rest at the sound of his name. This was Margaret, the sole daughter of Lord Killiecrankie, an embittered old Scot who had lost his fortune in the service of the Young Pretender. She had been born in Italy, where her father had loyally accompanied Charles Edward Stuart in his exile. When drink became his master's sole obsession, Killiecrankie forswore the Jacobite cause and returned to Scotland. His estates, with the exception of a ruined castle and a few acres of barren moor, had been confiscated, and he enjoyed no compensation, like Bonnie Prince Charlie, from the coffers of Versailles. In Bath, while nursing his gout, he met and married a prosperous brewer's widow, to whom his title was the prime attraction. Thus the wolf was kept from his door at the cost of his freedom. Dreaming ever of the wild Trossachs, he was compelled to lead a tame existence in Pulteney Street. Here he beguiled his boredom with playing on the bagpipe, to the aggravation of his wife and neighbours, for the barbaric strains could be heard throughout the length and breadth of that polite thoroughfare, to greet the dawn or sunset, according to the player's whim.

"If you would only play the spinet, my love," his spouse expostulated. " 'Tis infinitely more genteel."

"Gentility be hanged," growled Killiecrankie. "Don't provoke me. You should try to be a credit to your name and learn to relish it."

"I see no connection between my name and this instrument of torment."

He retorted by puffing out his cheeks and producing a loud wail that drove her from the room with her fingers in her ears. It was like the first birth-cry of Nature, swelling from beyond the far horizons of the world. A melody followed, importunate and vague, full of the pain, or the pleasure, of primeval things. The notes billowed into each other while he strutted up and down with a face turning purple. At such times the brewer's widow regretted her second marriage, but all her regrets vanished when she was called "Your Ladyship" in the Pump Room.

Her stepdaughter dreamed of

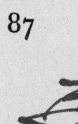

Italy, which she idealized through the haze of memory. When Isidore was introduced to her, she was drawn to him by this sentimental bond. But her northern ancestry was stamped on her face and figure. Her clear blue eyes, transparent skin, rose lips, and auburn ringlets —the Saxon loveliness made ethereal by a colder clime—were striking even at Bath where the type abounded. In her society Isidore found a tranquil enjoyment quite novel to him. Lisette had taught him how painful it was to experience passion unaccompanied by respect, to desire while doubting the value of the object. With Margaret his feelings were soothed, not electrified. He was content to inhale the lavender of her presence, and bear away its wholesome inspiration.

At first he fancied her cold, but the eloquent English that flowed from him with an unusual facility when he addressed her melted her by degrees, and she became suffused by a transitory glow. Her mouth had the flexible richness that ever indicates feeling; her eyes became bluer when he spoke of the Mediterranean; her utterance was delayed and musical, as of a heart just wakened from slumber.

Among other talents, she could sing very sweetly, and her Scottish ballads were often in demand. Remote as they were from the heady notes, the languid pauses and fiery rushes of Neapolitan music, Isidore thought they had the same pathos as his native songs. And when he saw her dance the Highland fling, he declared he preferred it to the *tarantella*. Margaret kindled him with an enthusiasm for Scotland and a warm interest in the House of Stuart. His King was living in exile too, like Charles Edward—but here he had to confess the resemblance ended, for no romantic achievement could be connected with Ferdinando, who had done little to command any chivalrous devotion.

How opportune for Isidore was this meeting! It gave him an image on which he could ponder with hope, instead of Lisette. Henceforth he resolved to abjure the false enchantments of vagrant desire. He would fall asleep with Margaret in his thoughts, she who had crossed his path like a winged angel. He would dwell upon the lofty promise, the rarefied delight, of which she seemed the herald. In short he had fallen seriously in love.

Day after day he drank the waters of Bath for her sake, since there was enough iron in his constitution for an armoury of weapons. In divers ways big and small, and by giving Margaret his undivided attention, he wished to prove the sincerity of his devotion.

She had been told that foreigners were indiscriminate philanderers, and she teased him cruelly about it. "You only wish to add me to your other conquests," she asserted.

"Please name them," he answered. "I defy you to mention a single lady to whom I have been more than polite, or who has been more than polite to me."

"My stepmother for one," she laughed. "Her Ladyship dotes on you."

"I have paid my respects to her out of tender regard for you, and I'm sure she's under no misapprehension."

He was gratified to hear that he was in the dame's good graces. The truth was that Lady Killiecrankie was itching to be rid of her stepdaughter, as of a young rival who shattered her self-esteem. Margaret's presence drew attention to that plebeian origin which it was her chief purpose to conceal, but she was too close-fisted to make a material provision for her. The lack of a dowry and her Catholic faith had discouraged English suitors. Having kept house for her father during his years of widowhood, Margaret was a constant reminder of his lost independence.

Thus Isidore's attentions were encouraged by the second Lady Killiecrankie and her gouty lord, and he came to be treated as one of the family. All Italians were counts, but this one was a prince; he was evidently a man of consequence in his own country. Few Italians were rich, but this one was reputed to have an income of 200,000 *lire* and forty horses in his stables, more than adequate for a girl of Margaret's simple tastes. The sooner he proposed the better, said her stepmother.

But Margaret could not make up her mind. Her stepmother's very eagerness restrained her. Mere names and social position were a very false standard of merit, she objected. She must put Isidore to the test. Had not the Italians a horrible proverb, "Matrimony is the tomb of love"? Besides, how vast was the difference between the love born of capricious tenderness and that fortified by principle and ennobled by intellectual sympathies! Margaret would only concern herself with the latter. So she kept her suitor dangling.

Isidore confessed that Bath, with its regular hours

and routine, would have been purgatory without her. In the morning he accompanied her dutifully to the Pump Room to hold her lap-dog, while she sipped the waters because it was the thing to do; after breakfast he sauntered with her on the parades; at night he was her partner in duets or the quadrille.

At intervals he sighed frequently, wept copiously, composed strings of sonnets, quoted Petrarch and Tasso, and sang serenades at her window.

One evening, during a rout at Lady Killiecrankie's, he looked for Margaret and heard that she was indisposed, suffering, as her stepmother explained, from a monthly megrim. "But it will surely not harm her to see you," she added with a smirk.

After a nervous knock at the door he rushed into Margaret's boudoir, the perspiration standing in large drops on his forehead, and an expression of impetuous despair about his eyes and mouth. He appealed to Margaret with great solemnity to answer frankly a question he intended to ask. Then, fixing his piercing eyes upon her face, he bade her tell him if she were betrothed to another.

Margaret could not speak for a minute or two from astonishment, and when she answered him, it was with an emphatic negative. Still he paced the chamber with a frantic air, indulging in an impassioned strain of which Margaret could grasp but little. In the midst of his harangue he called her a flint-hearted flirt, a cold native of a hyperborean clime, one who could not understand the emotions of a warm-blooded Italian.

"How well Tasso describes a lover!" he exclaimed.

"*Brama assai, spera poco, e nulla chiede:* he yearns much, hopes little, and asks for nothing."

"Ask and you shall receive," said Margaret quietly.

Isidore thought he would suffocate with joy. He knelt at her feet and sobbed, "I ask for you."

"I am yours," she murmured. "Take me back to Italy."

Isidore seized her hand and covered it with kisses. Margaret did not withdraw it, though it was wringing wet, for the kisses were mingled with tears of tenderness. He put his arm round her waist and drew her with gradual pressure to his heart. Trustfully she rested her head on his shoulder; both were silent; time flew. Suddenly his lips touched hers and a single flame ran through them simultaneously.

Their marriage was solemnized privately in Bath. Isidore did not take his bride to Italy at once. Something seemed to whisper to him that his misfortunes were not yet over. He dreaded returning to Naples, where he had no friends or kindred spirits. In Britain he had every reason to feel at home. His banker continued to remit vast sums of money; his estates were in the hands of capable administrators; and now that he was married he wished to live in peaceful domesticity with the woman he adored. Among the Scottish poems Margaret had read to him, none made a deeper impression than the lines:

> "*To make a happy fireside clime*
> *For weans and wife—*
> *Is the true pathos and sublime*
> *Of human life.*"

He went to Scotland for his honeymoon. He had promised to restore his father-in-law's ruined castle, which gave him a pretext to prolong his sojourn.

Margaret was soon with child, and her father did not wish her to leave Scotland before it was born. While in Edinburgh she was brought to bed of a boy under circumstances of exceptional danger and difficulty. As in the case of Isidore's birth, Margaret's labours were cruelly protracted, and the pangs increased without bringing the crisis exacted by Nature. The doctor interrupted Isidore in his bath and begged him to come and support his suffering wife, also revealing the sad truth that he doubted the possibility of saving both mother and child.

"Think only of the mother," exclaimed Isidore. At the same time, half dried, he ran to Margaret, and tenderly embracing her, exhorted her to courage and patience. But when the infant began to be delivered Isidore could not endure the scene another minute. He let fall Margaret's limp hand that he had clasped in his and rushed from the bedroom, pale as death, and almost out of his senses.

Every other instant he sent for news of Margaret and as soon as he heard that the child was born, he flew back and embraced her with delirious joy. The child remained at first without signs of life, and was of a greenish hue. Isidore glanced at it with distaste, saying not a word, and devoted his full attention to Margaret.

A few drops of brandy were blown by a quill into the infant's mouth while two maids rubbed the palms of his hands, massaged his body and covered it up with warm napkins. At length a faint cry was heard; it grew louder and louder. Isidore burst into tears and embraced his son, whose birth now appeared to him the summit of good fortune.

In the meantime, Lord Killiecrankie was playing his bagpipe in an adjoining chamber. Every man child of his family had been born to the sound of the pibroch, he declared: it was an ancient tradition that ensured continuity.

The old laird caroused all night with members of his clan, and died of an apoplexy in the morning. In Naples his death would inevitably have been associated with the birth of his grandchild, and to some extent it was. His delight had banished prudence. After exhausting his heart and lungs with inflating the leathern bag and pressing the air into the pipes with his elbow, he had quenched his thirst with an overdose of punch.

Margaret was not told of her bereavement until she was out of danger, but it cast a shadow over the first year of her marriage.

The child was to be christened Charles Edward, after the Young Pretender, for Margaret was still a Jacobite at heart.

"With submission, madam, there's no cranny for doubt that he's the son of his father," said her maid, and her words were too true.

Not only was Charles Edward a tiny image of his papa, but he had the same extraordinary eyes. They looked too old for any child, and far too knowing. A Neapolitan would have said without hesitation that

the fatal influence was to be carried on in the Prince's masculine line. The Scots were only superstitious about devils, ghosts, fairies, brownies, witches, warlocks, spunkies, kelpies, elf-candles, dead-lights, wraiths, apparitions, cantraips, giants, enchanted towers and dragons, but they appeared to be ignorant of that special fascination which was so dreaded in Naples. The "bonnie wee bairn's" tendency to smash whatever he touched was ascribed to mere animal spirits. The breakage of objects on which he merely looked was less easy to account for; glass, crockery and even furniture would suddenly crack in his presence. And it was noticed that his breath left a thick brown stain on the mirrors in his vicinity. But he became less destructive after his baptism.

No child yelled more at the font; his lungs were developed out of proportion to his age. He could sing a spirited version of "Scots wha hae wi' Wallace bled" while still in his cradle.

Since her father's death, Margaret's nostalgia for Italy increased. There was no reason to repair the castle now, she objected, for she would never cross its threshold: the place was gloomy and damp and infested with ghosts. It was situated in a country where savage streams tumbled over savage mountains, thinly speckled with savage flocks, which starvingly supported as savage inhabitants. Raeburn had painted a portrait of Lord Killiecrankie in Highland costume, his dour face and defiant figure set in a similar landscape. All critics agreed that it was one of Raeburn's grandest achievements, "bringing to mind visions of stirring days, great victories and noble defeats, and epitomizing the character of Highlanders and the Highlands." Isidore commissioned him to paint Margaret as well.

Margaret gave Raeburn innumerable sittings, and though she did not fidget, he had unusual difficulty with the portrait. Even the paints seemed to get muddled on his palette. He had begun with the brush as usual, since he never drew his heads or figures with chalk. But in spite of his accuracy of eye and hand, the result was strangely wooden.

The picture allowed Raeburn no rest. When it was nearly finished he conceived a dislike for it and began it all over again. Isidore sat watching him the while, and as Raeburn painted standing, he asked him if he were not fatigued. Just then the artist grew conscious of a cramp, and he was forced to sit down. He studied Margaret for a minute more and said: "I'm familiar enough with her Ladyship's features to paint them from memory. I dinna ken why but I canna paint them noo."

The portrait was completed without the model in Raeburn's George Street studio, yet it was a superb evocation of her beauty. She was depicted in a white muslin dress, cut low at the neck and fastened at the waist with a white satin bow. Over her gown she wears a cinnamon satin coat with long sleeves and tassels, and she stands beneath an oak. Her left arm rests on a branch, and she holds a volume of Burns's poems. The light of the Highland glens falling over the right shoulder models the soft, round cheeks and the fine, clear-cut nose. The wistful eyes, the parted lips, and the natural poise of the head express not only aristo-cratic beauty, but national character. It is a Scottish masterpiece, and though fashions have changed it still excites the admiration of those who see it in California, where it now hangs in a millionaire's collection.

As Margaret was expecting another child, Isidore made this a further pretext for postponing his departure.

She sat half the day at an embroidery frame by a large bow-window. Her needle faultlessly reproduced on canvas the picture she was copying, a view of Vesuvius. Her thoughts followed her work and floated beyond it to the scene of her future. Isidore had told her so little about his life in Naples. Considering his flow of speech on other subjects, this reserve was beginning to puzzle her. Except for communications with his banker and steward, he seemed cut off from his country. This might be explained by the King's continued exile; all the same, she wondered if Isidore had some other reason for keeping away. . . .

When she was not embroidering, Margaret lay coiled in a corner of a sofa, with her face half covered by a veil. Since her father's death she was seldom without this nun-like adornment. Her Scottish neighbours called it affectation, but she cared nothing for their society and consulted only her own wishes in costume as in weightier matters. With Isidore she always conversed in Italian, and together they devoured *Pastor Fido* and *Orlando Furioso*.

Isidore revelled in this cloistered domesticity. Nothing happened in the daily round beyond leisurely talk and a little landscape gardening. He was idle with a perfectly clear conscience. This time his wife's pregnancy affected him far more than it did her, and when the babe was born he had excruciating pains. Apart from being distressed by her husband's groans, Margaret did not suffer in the least.

Their second child was a daughter named Helen,

who already promised to blend the best of Scottish and Italian features. It was a picture of surpassing loveliness to see mother and children together. Isidore wanted Raeburn to paint it, but the artist politely refused, recommending him to Sir Thomas Lawrence.

THE Republican government's threat to confiscate the property of absent landlords forced Isidore to hurry back to Naples.

He had been absent five years, but he had not been forgotten. His neighbours trembled at his name, yet no one dared refuse his invitations. He and Margaret were extremely hospitable and entertained their guests with the utmost magnificence. Those who were young, amusing and enterprising flocked moth-like to the halls and galleries of the Pizzofalcone palace, which had been reopened and redecorated in Grecian and Gothic styles, attracted by the peculiar Northern charm and originality of the Princess, who introduced such novelties as Scottish tartans, bagpipes and the Highland reel.

The rule of Napoleon's elder brother Joseph Bonaparte was benevolent but dull, and any diversion was welcomed by a bored, impecunious society. Margaret's appearance was in itself a diversion. She always wore a different kind of drapery about her head and a dazzling variety of combs, tiaras and marabou feathers supported by diamond clasps. Elaborate curls were disposed on her forehead or in bands behind the ear; her hair was arranged in an intricate manner, the locks piled one by one, to form an auburn pyramid. Her cameo brooches and buckles were enormous in contrast with her waist. Her arms were bare or covered with the tightest of sleeves, and her petticoats were short to display her feet in sandalled shoes with open-worked stockings.

All the women were agog to know what she would wear next, while the men speculated on her history and antecedents. Had she married the Prince for love or money—in ignorance of his fatal repute or with open eyes, mustering all her courage to share his destiny?

So far she seemed to have escaped the contagion. Everything about her bade defiance to melancholy.

She was so cheerful and easy-going that she was irresistible to all who wanted sympathy. Her beauty

far exceeded that of Emma Hamilton, for whom she was often mistaken by the general public. Wherever her phaeton stopped she was mobbed like the magnificent ex-nursemaid with cries of, *"Bella, com' è bella! Pare la Santa Vergine!"* ("Beautiful, how beautiful she is! She seems the Holy Virgin!") And her little son and daughter were compared with celestial angels. But whereas Emma Hamilton had "the ease of a barmaid, not of good breeding," Margaret had the polished ease of a princess. Evidently she was a counter-charm to her husband's Evil Eye, which became powerless in her company.

Isidore was content to remain in the background, exclusively preoccupied with his wife's happiness and the education of his children. His sinister influence seemed to have dwindled since marriage, but it was observed by winning card-players that their luck would change if he stood near them, and once, when he praised the fish at a banquet, it began to stink so abominably that it had to be removed.

But these were trifles, and any reasonable man outside Naples would have given Isidore the benefit of the doubt. His estates prospered; he was a generous landlord and charitable to the poor, whom Margaret set out to physic with soap and soup as well as medicine.

Within the palace that had formerly been so tomb-like Margaret created a carnival atmosphere, in which her guests masqueraded in all manner of thoughts and feelings, and enjoyed the excitement of dressing up so much that for the moment they believed themselves to be what they pretended. She had a way of slipping ideas into conversation which other people developed; and even frivolous things and persons seemed to seethe with significance; the misanthropic became full of chivalry, the prosaic full of poetry, and the mediocre full of genius.

As his children grew up Isidore spent much time in cultivating their minds. With Charles Edward he read the best Latin and Italian authors, and taught him to reverence learning. He believed that knowledge should be imparted through the eyes, by visits to historic monuments, instead of from text-books. Virgil, Plutarch and Tacitus were illustrated by excursions in the neighbourhood, every step of which is classic ground, the birthplace of Cicero and Tasso and the tomb of Virgil. The latter leads not only to the infernal region of pristine legend, but also to the glorious age of Augustus. For Virgil had known the principal personages of that age and witnessed its greatest events. He had been the friend of Mæcenas, Sallust, Cornelius Nepos, Catullus and Horace; he had been the master of Propertius, Ovid and Tibullus.

"That was the golden age," said Isidore. "Now we only live in an age of gold."

A stone was raised at a small distance from the tomb, and on it was detailed the medicinal values of the adjacent baths of Baiæ and Pozzuoli and the antiquity of Virgil's remains. Charles Edward read the inscription in a clear, shrill voice which was strangely moving in that desolate place: "Mantua gave me birth; Calabria snatched me away; Parthenope holds my relics. I sang of meadows, of tilled fields and of heroes. Lo! the stones that cover my ashes are crowned by laurel which seldom grows on the soil of Pausilipum. Should my tomb crumble away, the laurel that will ever spring from my ashes will be an eternal monument to Maro's fame."

The sanctuary was reached by a ruined stairway overgrown with ivy and myrtle. Though the urn containing Virgil's ashes had been removed, the picturesqueness of the site was a greater stimulant than a schoolroom to a precocious boy of six.

"A few crusty pedants," said Isidore, "pretend that this was not Virgil's tomb. As if Augustus would allow his favourite poet to be buried outside Naples!"

After plucking a branch of laurel from the mausoleum, Isidore read the sixth book of the *Æneid* to his children, explaining that the horribly sublime scenery described there, the cavern of the sibyl, Lake Avernus and Acheron, were borrowed from the environs of Cumæ and Pozzuoli, which they had just visited.

Each landmark added a fresh subject to these

history lessons. Little Charles Edward was insatiable for catacombs, and Isidore took him to many. They entered the subterranean caves of the Church of San Gennaro and explored them to the extent of two miles and a half. Amid the human ashes, broken coffins and skeletons, Charles Edward danced with glee. He wanted to unravel the meanings of all the Greek inscriptions lying about, and he was thrilled by one recording the ravages of a pestilence in 1020. "When shall we have another pestilence?" he asked his father anxiously. "That was such a long time ago! Do you think we shall have one again?"

"It is unlucky to speak of such things," replied Isidore, seized by a sense of foreboding. . . .

But Charles Edward had discovered some paintings of Christians who had suffered martyrdom, and he asked if he could take them home to adorn his bedroom. For a while he vanished; then Isidore found him rummaging among marble fragments behind the tombs of the first Neapolitan bishops. He refused to leave the place until Isidore promised to take him back on the morrow.

At the age of nine Charles Edward's erudition was amazing; he had become an assiduous collector of Latin epitaphs, and his chief amusement was to compose them for his tutors and pet animals. Though Margaret did not approve of this pastime, Isidore thought it kept him out of mischief. "These innocent exercises," he said, "will train his mind to habits of good grammar and neat epithet, and keep him pure from every form of vice."

"You know best, dear," said Margaret, "but I hope they won't make him morbid."

One of Charles Edward's neatest epitaphs was composed for King Joachim Murat, who was dethroned and executed a few months later.

Except for one anxious week when a revolt of the *lazzaroni* was feared, 1815 was a felicitous year for Naples. Admiral Lord Exmouth arrived in May with four sail of the line, while Murat escaped in disguise on a Danish merchant vessel. Murat had been comparatively popular. During his reign he had increased the number of proprietors and promoted the agricultural energy of the people; the national revenue had been doubled and the debt halved. But Murat was a Frenchman none the less, and the Neapolitans preferred their own King Ferdinando, whom they regarded as one of themselves. The *lazzaroni* were an unruly element at the best of times, and the British Admiral landed marines to support the civic guard, a formation of the most respectable citizens to keep order.

For three days the city was under martial law. There were patrols of armed men in every street; the shops were all bolted and barred, and a stillness unique in Naples prevailed, which was only interrupted now and then by the challenging of patrols to stragglers after dark. Gradually the *lazzaroni* grew bolder and held secret meetings at which they planned to break open the prisons again and release their confederates. Fortunately, their plot was discovered. Twenty-two were fired upon and a hundred lost their lives.

On the twenty-third of May, Prince Leopold, the King's second son, entered Naples at the head of fifteen thousand Austrians. He received a tremendous ovation. The balconies of all the houses in the main streets were decorated, and the air was perfumed with the quantity of bouquets showered from the fairest hands of Naples on their deliverers as they marched towards the royal palace.

Margaret and Helen were cheered by the troops, who halted below their balcony, rapt by the vision of these Archangels. There was a fierce scramble for every flower they flung. Prince Leopold remained longer than the others, his eyes riveted on the two ladies, and he was observed to blow them a kiss and put a posy in his bosom.

Isidore did not appear. He had taken umbrage because he had not been invited to command the civic guard.

That evening the whole city was illuminated, and the streets were thronged with revellers long past midnight. Great was the change which twenty-four hours had effected. The preceding night distrust and fear had reigned, every house was a fortification, and most people closed their eyes with the dread of never opening them again. But now every door was open, every window was a blaze of light, and elation was apparent on every face.

The most liberal and generously worded proclamations had been issued, and as the King seemed likely to profit by the lessons of recent adversity, the Neapolitans had reason to think that their country would be one of the happiest in Europe. The King made his solemn entry from Portici on the seventeenth of June amid air-rending acclamations, since the Queen, whom all detested, was no longer with him. A royal salute was fired from the fleet upon Ferdinando's colours being hoisted on the castle of Sant' Elmo and the sea-forts of Uovo and Nuovo.

Soon after this Isidore was restored to many of his ancestral posts and privileges, such as Honorary Grand Majordomo Major to the King, thanks to the immediate favour which Margaret won at Court.

But a stunning blow now came to fulfil Isidore's worst forebodings. Charles Edward was snatched away by a death as gruesome as it was untimely.

Though a chip of the old block, the boy's Evil Eye was no match for his papa's: such was the general verdict.

Charles Edward's passion for catacombs led him to be immured in one of them. He spent so much time burrowing among tombs in vaults and subterranean passages that his frequent absence from home passed unnoticed and seldom caused alarm. Isidore had continued to encourage his archæological bent, despite the objections of Margaret, who did not care to think of her son rummaging mole-like under the ground. His tutors could never keep pace with him once he had scented another sarcophagus or urn. He was so swept away by enthusiasm that he was deaf to their summons and oblivious even of the calls of Nature. For hours at a time he would disappear with his lantern down crumbling corridors. Often he would indulge in an orgy of digging, to reappear at dinner with a freshly polished skull or collection of choice teeth, ribs and thigh bones. These fragments of skeletons were his especial pride; he mounted them himself with great skill and kept them in a glass cabinet near his bed.

Isidore beamed when he described his latest finds, discussing with relish their anatomical peculiarities and their probable origins. His family had produced no scholar of note for a century or more, and Charles Edward was something of a genius in this respect. Isidore was not so pleased, however, when Charles Edward recited to him a Latin epitaph which he had composed to adorn his own grave. "It is gracefully worded but a trifle premature," he said. And Margaret scolded Charles Edward for harbouring such thoughts. "You see where all this archæology is driving him," she complained. "The boy is becoming unpleasantly morbid. It would be better if he learned a little tact."

Charles Edward apologized. "I thought you might care to know in advance what sort of epitaph I'm capable of providing for you," he explained. "Of course, it was not intended to be final. I expect to improve my style under your tuition, Papa."

Isidore patted his head and told him not to worry. "There is plenty of time for that, dear boy, later on. At least I hope so."

"I hope so too, Papa. I've also been looking out for

a nice tomb-stone, a genuine antique one of Parian marble, really well carved. Porphyry might be more suitable. It is infinitely harder. The drawback is that it doesn't show inscriptions so clearly."

"This conversation must stop at once," said Margaret. "I refuse to listen to another word on the subject. Run off to bed, Charles Edward, before you make me angry. Try to think of something jolly for a change!"

Margaret sighed, but she could not influence Charles Edward in any way. He had inherited none of the Killiecrankie characteristics. Fortunately, Helen had.

Aware of his mother's disapproval, Charles Edward became secretive about his excursions, and one day he vanished in the depths of a catacomb beyond recall. In attempting to move a marble slab which had struck him as the perfect ornament for his father's tomb, the slab had fallen on top of him, crushing him backwards into a newly opened grave and clamping him down there like a trap-door and wall combined.

His tutor had heard a cry, but its echo was swallowed long before he could reach it. The underground passage was so uniformly dark and it was blocked by so much rubble that he had to give up the search when the oil of his lamp ran out. A custodian and some labourers came to his assistance. By the opening of the main vault one of the latter declared he could hear a muffled moaning. Each being provided with a lantern, they wandered down various sections of the catacomb. A scream was heard, but it was like a will-o'-the-wisp; none could determine whence it came. After several hours one of the workmen noticed the freshly crumbled earth where the slab had stood. This provided a clue and all started feverishly digging.

Charles Edward was found suffocated among a heap of old bones. Apparently he had not been killed at once; from the convulsed attitude of the corpse, he had struggled with all his might to push the slab away from him. His hands were still clenched and bleeding and the fingernails torn, but he was otherwise intact, except for some minor fractures and abrasions. The inflamed eyeballs protruded from their sockets with a moonstone phosphorescence.

Charles Edward's tutor could not muster the courage to tell the Prince and Princess. He went and drowned himself in Lake Fusaro instead. The labourers broke the news crudely in hopes of a reward. Charles Edward was buried in the family vault under the same slab of marble he had selected for his father.

Isidore and Margaret were prostrated. They mourned a whole year in mutual anguish, until Helen pathetically reminded them that "those whom the gods love die young," and they realized that they owed it as a duty to their *débutante* daughter to cease mourning the dead and turn towards the living.

"Charles Edward may be more fortunate than we," said Isidore with religious resignation. "Evidently it was God's will. Let us mention it no more."

Helen had blossomed like a tea-rose under her mother's wing, and at the age of sixteen her beauty was the cynosure of the Two Sicilies. The first question asked of any newcomer was: had he seen the enchanting

Princess? Nothing could exceed the delicacy of her features or the brilliance of her tints. Her very pace seemed nobler than that of other mortals. She moved, high stepping, like the sublimation of a thoroughbred unicorn. A fairer and taller version of her mother, she was called another Helen of Troy. All the young men of Naples, and most of the old ones, thought themselves poets at the sight of her. They showered her with sonnets and deafened her with serenades, but there was only one whose emotion she could reciprocate. As luck would have it this was the sole son of one of Parthenope's wealthiest patricians, but he was also a notorious profligate.

At the age of nineteen Count Carlino Forabosco had wrought such havoc among the ladies that he had acquired the nickname of Wild Solomon, which inferred that he had as many mistresses as the Biblical king had wives.

Isidore delivered a diatribe against the depravity of the younger generation whenever Carlino was mentioned—to no purpose so far as Helen was concerned.

Was it due to magnetism spiritual or physical, or to a demon of perversity? Was it because she had formed so high an opinion of Carlino's merits, or because she had heard so much scandal? The fact remains that she fell in love with the only suitor to whom her father objected. Nor was it one of those fleeting fancies that are kindled by caprice and killed by criticism. It was a consuming passion, increased by every obstacle and watered with secret tears.

Their first opportunity to speak to each other was at a display of fireworks to celebrate the anniversary of her parents' wedding. A triumphal arch had been erected opposite the palace, and over and around and within it Roman candles, rockets and cascades broke into breathless combinations of shape and colour and sound. Helen was standing beside Count Carlino on a balcony, but neither of them looked at the spectacular fountains of fire which reddened the night. In half shadow they stood and yearned towards each other; Helen slim and pale, with a rippling coronet of hair too dense for the breeze to ruffle, Carlino tall and tense, his eyelashes and side-whiskers flashing like quicksilver against his olive skin.

They did not hear the explosion and swish of the rockets, the shrill violins of the orchestra within, or the salvoes of applause when the mouths of two statues spat bright bouquets of sparks. They could only hear the hammer of their hearts, which beat as one. In their secret selves already they were united. Helen shivered as she felt herself melting under the flame of his eyes. He slid a hand down one of her cool bare arms and gripped her fragile wrist.

That gesture conquered her before he spoke. Though he gripped her painfully, she did not cry out. She stood limp and impassive, while he murmured, "I adore you."

Then a rocket fell sputtering at her feet, and her father appeared and begged her to go indoors. "Why, of all the follies!" he exclaimed. "To stand exposed to the night air in your flimsy dress without a shawl! You'll catch your death of cold. Your mother and I have been searching for you everywhere. . . ."

But Helen contrived to have one dance with Carlino before she retired to dream of him, and he whispered, "I am yours for ever. Never believe what else you hear of me. I love you until death."

It was but a whisper and the breeze dispelled it, yet Helen heard it again and again, more desperate, more beseeching. Those words gave her strength to steel herself against all resistance, a strength which she needed during the next few months.

Helen had always been candid: she concealed nothing from her parents. Now she told them that she had met the only man she would ever marry.

Though Isidore doted on his daughter, he was opposed to her marriage with an unprincipled rake. He taxed all his ingenuity in an effort to destroy her naïve illusions. Every day he renewed the onslaught, and he made a special point of acquainting her with the latest exploits of which Count Carlino was the villain. No spiritual or domestic vows were too sacred for this ruthless beast of prey. He had got both a mother and daughter with child simultaneously, and had seduced a bevy of nuns into the bargain. He showed no respect for age or rank; from duchesses to chamber-maids, he tumbled them all in the same determined fashion, casting them aside when he had sown his oats.

This catalogue of iniquities had no effect on Helen. Carlino was misjudged, she retorted, because he was built on a nobler scale than the rest of mankind; he had deeper passions and a more generous heart. She was sure that she could manage him. All her Caledonian ancestry came swelling to the fore.

HELEN loved Carlino with an intensity of which her parents could not have thought her capable, for she was hardly more than a child and her passion was that of a tenacious woman.

When Isidore tried threats and cajoleries, she created a scene which was heard all over the palace. She threw herself at Isidore's feet, and amid a torrent of tears cried out that she could not live without Carlino.

Isidore remained gentle but firm. It was the fancy of a love-sick girl, he thought; the fever was bound to cool. Both he and Margaret argued with her to the point of exhaustion. Helen refused to listen. She repeated again and again, like the words of a rosary, "I simply cannot exist without Carlino."

Her health began to suffer. Her cheeks grew wan, her eyes lost their lustre, and she was permeated by a listless melancholy. She rarely smiled, and then it was like the feeble glimmer of a winter sun. As the weeks dragged into months she seemed in danger of pining away. Her parents were so worried that they summoned the family physician and asked him for a complete diagnosis. The doctor was unusually honest. He told them bluntly that this was not a case for medicine. The young Princess's ailment was due to moral causes. Some hidden despair was lurking behind her languor. If she continued to decline it might easily prove fatal. Had Helen any secret? he inquired.

The secret in question was too well-known to Isidore, but he stood his ground for another fortnight, while Helen grew weaker every day. She rejected even the most delicate food, and the doctor warned Isidore that he would assume no further responsibility.

Margaret implored Isidore to relent. "We must rely on her natural strength of character," she said. "Heaven knows she has already given us proof of it, and I am sure she will succeed in reforming that naughty boy. Don't forget that she is half a Killie-crankie. She will make his morality her vocation."

"No girl has ever done that for any man. I'm afraid his morality doesn't concern her at all."

"Helen is different. She'll persuade him to settle down. I hear that he has also been quite ill. . . ."

"I'll warrant from another cause," said Isidore.

"We should try to see the best side of him, for Helen's sake. Unless his love were genuine he wouldn't have been so persistent. All those babies are the relics of early entanglements, before he considered matrimony. I dare say the women were to blame. You can't deny that he is ornamental, and I have seen many a matron who should know better set her cap at him. He has been very humble and penitent in his inquiries. His father promises to make a handsome settlement if you will reconsider your decision."

"His father knows that she's rich enough to need no settlement," said Isidore.

Though he dreaded confiding his daughter's future to such a libertine, he could find no alternative. Finally, he told Helen that as her life was dearer than the whole world to him, he would agree to her marriage with Count Carlino Forabosco.

The news produced a miraculous recovery. The roses returned to her cheeks, her blue eyes sparkled again, and she smiled with an angelic radiance. She threw both arms around her father's neck and promised him not only to live, but to be happy.

Isidore shook his head despondently. He could foresee scant happiness from a satyr as a son-in-law. Only yesterday he had heard that Count Carlino had saddled his sister's governess with triplets. . . . Having given his solemn word, he allowed Helen to communicate with her lover.

Carlino appeared in her ante-room as soon as he received the letter. Being convalescent, Helen was reclining before a long gilt looking-glass which re-assured her that she had lost none of her beauty. Dressed in a robe of floating muslin which was hardly whiter than her skin, she looked like the Snow Princess. Her eyes were enlarged and intensified in circles of blue from so many sleepless nights, and they were blurred with tears when Carlino knelt before her and wept in a paroxysm of devotion. Sobbing for joy, she twined her arms round his neck, pressing him close to her palpitating bosom. "My Carlino, my love, my husband," she murmured hoarsely.

In a delirium of delight, Carlino swore by the Virgin and all the saints that he would never leave her.

Isidore retreated muttering to himself. Had he stayed a minute longer he too would have burst into tears. He clasped Margaret's hand for comfort, grumbling, "It's irretrievable. But I don't like it. I still don't like it. I have been forced to yield against my better judgment."

"You have acted as a magnanimous father. We would have lost her otherwise."

"I hope I don't live to rue it."

"Don't be a pessimist. Youth will have its way."

After all the trouble his refusal had caused, Isidore thought that the marriage had better be early. The ceremony was arranged for three weeks later, which allowed sufficient time for the usual formalities.

While Helen and Margaret were busy selecting the *trousseau*, Isidore was flooded with anonymous letters attacking his future son-in-law. These came from jilted girls who described him as a faithless lover, from disconsolate mothers who described him as a heartless parent. He had in each case seduced and deserted the writer and broken every pledge. Though the phraseology differed—several were uneducated and supplied their want of grammar with crude expletives—the gist was always the same, a chorus of indignation which multiplied Isidore's worst misgivings. But Isidore knew that it would kill Helen if he revoked his promise, so he made a supreme effort to silence the groans of his conscience. In the meantime, Helen scintillated with vivacity, as if she had drunk some invigorating potion, basking in the sunlight of her newly discovered joy.

The wedding festivities were regal, and those privileged to witness the ceremony were unanimous in declaring that throughout the Two Sicilies it would be impossible to find a more harmonious couple. The same night a banquet and ball were given at the Pizzofalcone palace, and Isidore's eye was dimmed by the general revelry. The bridegroom was all smiling confidence and the bride all anticipation.

The young couple were too absorbed in each other to do justice to the banquet. But the guests, who despite their high pedigrees and outward pomp were mostly accustomed to a single meal *per diem*, stuffed themselves to burst buttons point and swept what they had no room for into leather pockets especially devised for that purpose.

Isidore had held several conferences with his *maître d'hôtel*, head cook, roaster, pastrycook, confectioner and cellarman, at which every dish and wine were debated in advance.

"We must show the world that Naples can rival Paris in the culinary arts," he declared. Whatever happened, he could at least look back on his contribution without regret. Since he had a preference for poultry, he decided that poultry was to predominate. It was a dismal day for the birds on his estates. Though Isidore went to the coverts with his gun, the latter was superfluous. One look at the winged quarry sufficed; the majority dropped dead before he had fired a shot. It was equally dismal for the fish. Neither net nor hook were required, for as Isidore approached, the carp in his ponds floated up to the surface in shoals, gasping for air long before they were caught.

The result of this devastating excursion was roughly summarized in the following bill of fare: two grand soups of partridge and three thousand carps' tongues, two ordinary soups of bisque of pigeons and cock's combs, four side soups of hashed capons, partridge and lentils, stuffed chicken and boiled capon, quarter of veal and pigeon pie as grand *entrées*, fricassee of pigeon and salmi of partridge as ordinary *entrées*, six side dishes of roast partridge, braised pigeons, grilled turkeys, truffled chickens, whole and in hash, two large dishes containing plump capons, chickens, pigeons, partridges and pies, two dishes of woodcock, teal, young capons and partridges, and eleven vegetables, salads and omelettes, including the royal omelette of cock's combs and roes of carp, besides creams, foies-gras and truffles, rissoles and beignets and dessert in proportion.

A Pulcinella pantomime was performed in an open-air

theatre outside the palace, with tiers of raised seats for the audience; and a hundred illuminated boats, each with a group of guitar players, rowed up and down by the shore of the Chiaia. Unfortunately several tiers of seats collapsed under the weight of too many spectators. Over a hundred were trampled to death in the ensuing panic and a thousand were severely injured.

Isidore was blamed as usual, instead of the carpenters, and the accident was considered a bad omen for the married pair. But within the palace all went smoothly. A few suffered from indigestion as a result of over-indulgence, but Isidore could hardly be blamed for that, and the ball itself was a memorable success. Helen and Carlino danced the polonaise like figures in a trance, and if eyes were endowed with voices theirs sang a rapturous duet.

It was early morning when the last guests departed, and the bride and groom were left with the Prince and Princess. Overcome by a fit of virginal shyness, Helen took refuge in her mother's arms, while Carlino pumped Isidore's hand so vigorously that he thought his wrist was broken. But it was a moment of such dynastic import that he forgot the pain. Our family will benefit from his vigour, he reflected; it is bound to fortify the stock. Beaming with satisfaction, he put an arm round each of the pair and kissed their foreheads. "Come, my dear children," he said benignly, "let me give you a father's blessing before you go to bed."

Piously the young couple knelt before him. First Isidore raised his hands to Heaven, then he lowered them tremulously over their bowed heads. He paused in search of inspiration and, not knowing how to express himself more Biblically, pronounced the words: "Increase and multiply!"

Having fulfilled this duty, Isidore's spirits began to flag, and he retired to his chamber in an abstracted mood. There Margaret soon joined him, in the fond belief that the bridal pair were putting his words into practice. Her only fear was that Carlino might exhaust her delicate child. She had whispered a few intimate counsels in Helen's ear. "You must allow him to take certain liberties on so privileged an occasion," she told her.

"I adore him so that I shall give him *carte blanche*," said Helen.

"But you must not appear too eager. *Surtout pas trop de zèle*, as Metternich said. It applies to love as well as politics. Bear that in mind, my darling."

"I'll try, Mamma, but it will be awfully hard."

Margaret could not repress a smile at the earnestness of Helen's tone. Her eyes were twinkling like stars when she bade her good night.

"I feel as if we were being married all over again," said Isidore. "Let us increase and multiply too. It is not too late."

"I'm very tired," said Margaret. "I must look a perfect frump."

"You have never looked lovelier. Come into my arms and I shall give you rest."

"You rascal," said Margaret. "You know you will give me nothing of the kind."

Now that she was in her thirties there was a mother-liness in Margaret's soft and ample contours which exerted a powerful charm over Isidore, who had not known a mother. He loved her more in her ripe maturity. She had the languid movements of a woman who was rather fully developed for her years, well aware that this healthy *embonpoint* became her. The calm gaze of her placid eyes, her gently rounded cheeks, full lips and alabaster bust evoked the height of summer before the harvest. And it was a Scottish summer, not a Neapolitan one, which rendered her more exotic in these surroundings. Isidore behaved as if it were the first night of his honeymoon.

Hence neither couple were visible till late in the day, when they assembled for a solid breakfast. Isidore and Margaret had gargantuan appetites, but the younger pair ate sparingly.

Helen flushed crimson on seeing her father; she lowered her eyes and stammered when she spoke. Never had she been so coy in look and gesture. Carlino, too, was oddly embarrassed when he greeted the Prince. As pale as Helen was pink, he hung his head listlessly, shuffled and fidgeted, tugged at his jacket, twisted his fingers, and spilled his food on the table-cloth. He seemed to have lost his buoyancy. His whole expression denoted strain, and his eyelids twitched and drooped. As these blushes and embarrassments appeared natural under the circumstances, Margaret and Isidore kept up a placid conversation about the weather.

The parents deemed it tactful to leave the young

lovebirds to themselves as much as possible and were not in the least surprised when they spent the rest of the day in their apartment. At dinner, however, they found them even more shy and reserved. Helen could not utter without a blush spreading over her cheek like wine in a glass of water, and Carlino's expression of strain amounted almost to a paralysis of the facial muscles. He perspired copiously and kept dabbing his forehead with his handkerchief.

Isidore and Margaret exchanged sympathetic smiles. Sensibility was the latest cult: that must account for it. They had never been quite so sensitive themselves. Who would have expected the dashing Count Carlino to behave like an awkward country swain? Evidently Helen had reformed him already. There was a suggestion of the hen-pecked husband in his obsequious stoop and downcast eyes when Helen glanced at him. And there was more than a hint of superciliousness in the curve of Helen's lip when he addressed her. She answered him curtly, with an arrogant toss of her curls. Yes, Carlino seemed crushed, almost sorry for himself. It was easy to see which had the upper hand.

Margaret was gratified by this transformation, which proved that she had not been mistaken about Helen's strength of character. After dinner Isidore announced that he and Margaret had decided to spend the next few days in the country. "We'll leave you to enjoy your happiness in freedom. The whole palace is at your disposal. And since 'music is the food of love,' I have engaged a band of musicians to play to you."

While he spoke an orchestra struck up an enchanting overture. The considerate parents bade them a fond farewell and drove off to their country villa, each preoccupied by private observations of an intimate nature, to which neither made any allusion during the long drive. Tingling memories of their own courtship returned to them in the moonlight. They found their own youth again amid the eternal youth of Nature, without any slurring sense of the passage of time.

A few days later, while Isidore and Margaret were taking their afternoon siesta, both were aroused by the rattle of carriage wheels. Not expecting visitors at this hour, they were astonished. A butler knocked at the door, followed by a running footman, who breathlessly announced that the Countess Forabosco was due to arrive. They did not have to wait long.

Helen's altered appearance gave both of them a start. Her face was as white and drawn as during her illness, her hair was dishevelled, and she tottered rather than walked, with a wild gleam in her eye. She rushed straight into her mother's outstretched arms and sobbed hysterically. It was a distressing sight, and her parents were at their wits' ends to discover the meaning of it. Isidore capered beside her

in a frenzy of anxiety, imploring her to explain what had happened. The more he questioned her, the more she sobbed, without uttering a word. At last a hideous thought occurred to him. "Oh, the monster," he bellowed. "Has he been unfaithful already?"

"Alas!" sighed Helen. "Would to Heaven he were capable of it!"

"Capable? What do you mean, dear? Pray do not keep us on the rack like this. Be brave and tell us the worst. We shall see that your wrongs are righted. What has happened to you since we left?"

There was a tense and throbbing silence in expectation of the thunderbolt. Then—"Nothing," she murmured, "nothing at all." The blushes spread from her face to her ivory neck.

"Nothing, dear daughter? Please be more lucid, child. I'm getting old, perhaps, but this is beyond my comprehension."

Helen glanced from her father to her mother like a startled doe. "It is something," she faltered, "which I could only tell Mamma."

"Come along, darling, and let us have a heart-to-heart talk," said Margaret. "Things are never so bad as they seem. You can tell me everything. I may be able to help you."

"I don't know if I dare," said Helen. "I feel so . . . so humiliated."

"Is it so very terrible?" asked Isidore.

"It is too dreadful for words, Papa."

"Then I shall have to go and shoot the villain."

"Oh, don't do that, Papa. He hasn't been cruel—in

fact, he has tried to be kind. But . . . I really can't put up with it any longer."

"It is no use being wise after the event, but I was wise before. I warned you that this cad would make you miserable."

"But not in the way you anticipated. How I wish I had taken your advice!" replied Helen meekly.

"Don't lose heart," said Margaret. "At your age one can nearly always find a remedy."

"I fear that in this case there is no remedy, Mother mine."

The melancholy bride yielded to her mother's persuasion. They retired arm in arm to the privacy of Margaret's bedroom. There the fantastic and incredible secret was revealed. The Don Juan of Naples, the hero of a thousand and one nights, the prancing stallion whose precocious career of paternity had caused Helen's parents such consternation, could not be called a husband in the real sense of the word— and this after one week's marriage to the girl he pretended to adore. The most extraordinary part of it was that Carlino's reputation as a ravisher had been far from false; on the whole, it had been underrated.

Margaret prescribed patience and tact.

"After waiting so long, Mamma? After dreaming such passionate dreams?"

"The situation is not nearly so bad as you had led me to fear. He loves you too much, and looks upon you as a holy being—a goddess on a pedestal. Perhaps you have been too high and mighty with him. He has never met a girl like you before, so beautiful and

brilliant and well-bred. He has only consorted with common maids-a-mischief. Consequently, he is petrified with respect, and there is a conflict between passion and his dread of displeasing you. But he is bound to return to his normal self after a while."

"But he's so clumsy and fumbling, Mamma. He tries and tries and all his efforts are futile. Nothing could be more *gauche* than his gestures, or more stupid than his face as he puffs and pants and calls me silly names. I'd rather he did not touch me. After a whole week I'm sick to death of it. He prevents me from getting any sleep. I've always been ticklish, and he can't help tickling me. He bites too. My neck and shoulders are all bruises. It's most uncomfortable."

"You had better sleep in a separate bed. That should bring him to his senses."

"I think he should consult a doctor," said Helen.

This was precisely what Carlino had done, but the pills and potions recommended had merely irritated his nervous system, exciting the mind without affecting the body. In his desperation, he had begun to blame Helen for his own frigidity.

Eventually Helen returned to Carlino with the best intention of following her mother's advice. But she could not resist human nature. Being in the full bloom of youth, she could not be content with a mere ornament for a husband. She kept her secret from the outside world, and made a gallant effort to be sprightly in public. But she yearned for children and, as time wore on, the prospect of motherhood grew more remote.

Carlino disguised his mortification with polite attentions that filled her with contempt, since she felt them to be insincere. She came to regard him as a tailor's dummy, a man of straw, and conceived an aversion almost amounting to hatred, which it was difficult not to show.

Isidore and Margaret pitied the poor children profoundly. They treated Carlino with unvarying kindness

132

and consideration. But the reformed rake's hypo-chondria oppressed the entire household. He became surprisingly pious, and went on frequent pilgrimages to wonder-working shrines and restorative baths. On the surface his health appeared excellent. Helen was envied by all her friends for so handsome and amiable a husband.

Three years elapsed without anything to break the spell of which Carlino was the victim. Towards the end of this period a strange rumour began to circulate. Countess Forabosco, who was generally considered a paragon of domestic bliss, was said to be seeking a divorce. This could only be achieved through an article in the Council of Trent, which provided for annulment in cases of impotence.

The rumour found few believers in the city of Naples. The ladies shrugged their shoulders at so extravagant an improbability, but the gentlemen insisted that there was no smoke without fire.

Was this the Nemesis lying in wait for profligacy? All the young libertines trembled and took note.

Helen had made a special application to the Roman tribunal of the Rota, which gave her case an unsavoury publicity. Everybody discussed and analysed the events which had followed her wedding. A fashionable philosopher drew the deduction that too ethereal a love, too lofty a sublimation of human passion, might result in a local numbness. The body, he alleged, was apt to take a vicious revenge on the mind. Soaring on the pinions of ecstasy, the spirit was all ardour, and the earth-bound flesh froze up in sheer resentment. But the ladies objected that Count Carlino had never been spiritually inclined. He had established himself early as a votary of Venus and Pan, of the earth earthy, in whose veins the blood of pagan ancestors predominated. One detail passed unobserved: the paternal blessing and the Biblical form in which it was invoked.

During the controversy that ensued, all the men ranged themselves on the side of the Countess and all the women on that of the Count. Naples was so divided by domestic feuds that it was practically in a state of civil war.

The intervention of Prince Isidore was overlooked in the heat of these discussions. The majority of husbands not only declared that Count Carlino was impotent, but that he had been so from the start. The wives protested that their menfolk were either absurdly prejudiced or hopeless imbeciles.

Helen was so dissatisfied that she braved appearing before a jury of doctors and midwives. It did not take them long to pronounce her as inviolate as Joan of Arc.

The Neapolitan husbands held a banquet to celebrate their triumph, at the end of which they seized hands and danced in a ring. Even so the ladies refused to yield. As is well known, when women have a fixed idea it is hard to drive it out. These would cling to their idea of the Count's compelling character until they were given palpable proof to the contrary. No doctor or midwife was infallible, said they, and Prince Pizzofalcone was wealthy enough to bribe any jury on behalf of his daughter.

Since the council of the Rota was not composed of women, it decreed that this marriage, which had never been consummated, was null and void. After the verdict, both Helen and Carlino were free to contract another marriage if they so desired. Carlino was so ashamed that he went off and joined the *Carbonari*, to prove his virility in other ways.

HELEN was not slow to take advantage of her emancipation. During the last year of her nominal marriage an eligible bachelor, the Marchese Luciano Caffarelli, had been paying her assiduous court, but she had too keen a sense of honour to admit, even to herself, that she returned his sympathy with interest. This reserve was admired even by those who had accepted lovers or *cavalieri serventi*, a custom which society then took for granted, and her wooer respected her all the more for it.

As soon as her marriage was annulled, the Marchese, who had been waiting on tiptoe to step into Carlino's shoes, hastened to offer his heart and hand to Helen. Both were accepted; and an announcement of their impending nuptials followed. This time Isidore could raise no objection. Since Helen had come of age she was entitled to her own choice.

Marchese Caffarelli had everything in his favour, including reputation. His genealogy was beyond reproach; he was affluent enough to be clear from mercenary motives; and he was aide-de-camp to Prince Leopold. Though no Adonis like his predecessor, for his skin was swarthy and his nose too inaccessible, he was eminently a man of parts, with a resplendent row of teeth. The match seemed suitable from every point of view. He had never been entangled in a vulgar intrigue, and his whole air was one of steadfast single purpose. Helen thought him restful and reliable, and her parents agreed.

A discreet period was allowed to elapse for the sake of convention, during which her fiancé was sent on a diplomatic mission to Vienna. He returned on the eve of his wedding, loaded with gifts which did credit to his taste. That which pleased Helen most was a minute harpsichord with a mechanical bird which popped out and trilled a Mozartian tune. The purity of the notes sounded like a prelude to a pastoral symphony.

If Helen was less rapturous than before her first marriage, she was far more serene, and after three tantalizing years with Carlino she had come to prefer serenity.

The nuptials were celebrated in private. This time there was neither a banquet nor a ball. The ceremony took place in the chapel of Isidore's country house, with only four witnesses beside the Prince and Princess. But, as on the previous occasion, Isidore could not refrain from making a speech after the wedding, which he intended to follow likewise with his blessing. The bride and bridegroom were rather bored by it, but they managed to listen with an air of deference until Isidore asked them to kneel. Suddenly Helen recoiled from her father as if he were about to strike her. "For Heaven's sake, Papa, not another word! Whatever you do, don't bless us."

Isidore was amazed by this outburst. Nevertheless, he insisted on accomplishing what he regarded as a parental rite.

Panic overcame Helen's filial respect. She seized her husband's arm and dragged him out of the room. So precipitous was her flight that Isidore did not see the twin horns that she made with both hands, in order doubly to avert her father's influence.

Having reached the safety of her nuptial chamber, Helen locked the door firmly behind her and turned the key twice to make sure. For even now the doldrums that had followed the hurricane of her girlish passion sent shivers down her spine.

Margaret was almost as nervous as her daughter lest family history should repeat itself, and she persuaded Isidore to return with her to the city. But when she saw Helen again her anxiety was dispelled. The bride was so radiant that there could be no doubt of a happy consummation. Helen told her that Luciano was a model of devotion. Nobody, she said, could be more pliant to her slightest whim. And he was a genuine man, as strong as he was gentle. He gave her all the right sensations. Even his nose had become an accessible and endearing feature.

Helen's happiness, so dearly won, was increased by

138

the prospect of maternity. Two months prematurely she gave birth to a boy who was prematurely developed. In one respect he startled even the midwife. She had never seen such precocious evidence of manhood. All the women gathered round his cradle in admiration. What a big little man! they exclaimed. An infant Hercules with extraordinary muscles, he resented being put into swaddling clothes and tore them to shreds immediately. But he was not otherwise ill-tempered, and his laughter was more frequent than his tears. Naturally, he became the idol of the household.

A handsome nurse from Procida was engaged to look after him. She wore mother-of-pearl ear-rings, a crimson bodice embroidered with gold, and a billowing skirt with silver fringes. The servants had orders to obey her implicitly and she was installed in a sumptuous nursery. It was a temple of pink marble, with a rococo pediment covered with frolicsome cupids.

The boy was christened Hercules, after his great-uncle who had been killed in the duel, and the name was appropriate. Margaret and Isidore doted on him, and his parents lavished all their affection on this prodigy. Within a year he could prattle quite comprehensibly and express his preferences with sportive bounds, as prompt at recognizing friends as he was critical of strangers. His father and grandfather were welcome to play with him at any hour. He always held out his chubby arms to them and greeted them with shouts of glee. But he showed an antipathy for other men. Already he evinced a partiality for the ladies.

So great was Isidore's attachment to his baby grandson that when the King proposed to send him on a distinguished mission he was reluctant to accept it. The purport of this was to congratulate King Charles X of France on the capture of Algiers.

Isidore's notoriety had stood in the way of his preferment at Court, and it was only at the instigation of his son-in-law that the King made this belated gesture as a consolation prize for past rebuffs. Having carefully weighed the odds, His Majesty decided that Isidore could do least harm in Paris. He had no love for the French, whatever their political complexion. They had started all these poisonous new ideas; besides, they had kept him out of Naples too long. Sending them the Evil Eye would be tit for tat.

But Isidore had grown indifferent to royal favour. It had come too late to flatter his self-esteem. "I am only a retired and retiring family man," he told his son-in-law. "I couldn't bear to be parted from Hercules for a single day. He's my beam of sunshine, the apple of my eye."

Luciano warned him that his refusal would offend the King and strengthen his detractors, most of whom were only too eager to perform so honourable a mission.

"What? Have I detractors?" asked Isidore incredulously. Luciano hemmed and hawed, not caring to enter into particulars. "The Court is full of jealous backbiters," he said. "I beg you to consider the consequences. If you reject the King's offer—a token of confidence all the more rare since you are a private gentleman without political affiliations—he will doubt your loyalty. His suspicions will reflect on your family. Fomented by our enemies, they will undermine our position at Court. We shall be accused of Jacobin tendencies. Since you were in Naples during the French occupation, they can perpetrate plenty of mischief."

Margaret urged him to go, if only to buy her some bonnets, and Helen wanted him to procure her a long list of Parisian novelties.

"It will do you good to rub the rust off," they said, and by loading him with commissions they persuaded him to accept. He left with a heavy heart. It was mid July in 1830, soon after the surrender of Algiers to the French.

Travelling in a state carriage drawn by six horses, with an escort of running footmen in gold lace and epaulettes, Isidore progressed at a speed of ten miles an hour when the roads were level, and he travelled night and day, so anxious was he to end his mission and return to Naples.

Twenty-four years had elapsed since his escapade with Lisette, of which France disagreeably reminded him. He cared so little for the scenery that he travelled with the blinds drawn. On the twenty-fourth of July he was informed that he had entered Paris.

Having bespangled himself with all the stars of Neapolitan orders which testified to his rank, he hastened to present his credentials at the Ministry of Foreign Affairs. Two days later, when he had fulfilled his errands for Margaret and Helen, he was received in solemn audience by the King of France.

Charles X was an ultra-Bourbon who was trying to restore the monarchy of Louis XIV, with the assistance of his short-sighted minister, Prince Jules de Polignac. The French deputies by a formal vote had just declared their lack of confidence in the Polignac ministry, and Charles X had retaliated by dissolving the Chamber and ordering a new election. "This is not a question of the Ministry, but of the Monarchy," he had pronounced. "Perform your duty," he told the electors, "and I will do mine."

Louis XIV had said: "I am the State." Charles X was practically saying: "I am the Ministry." The

result of the new elections was a large increase in the Opposition, so he determined on a virtual suspension of the Constitution. Czar Nicholas of all the Russias, an absolutist if ever there was one, had warned him to be careful, since nobody wanted another revolution. But Charles retorted: "Concessions ruined Louis XVI."

In the meantime, Talleyrand, who had done so much to obtain the recall of the Bourbons, had made this oracular judgment: "In 1814 the return of the Bourbons secured the repose of Europe. In 1830 or 1831 their departure will secure the repose of France."

But Charles and his reactionary ministers would not allow matters to be delayed until 1831. Even while Isidore was ushered into his presence, Charles was rubbing his hands over Polignac's latest *coup*. On the strength of a vague clause in the Charter which gave the King power to issue ordinances for the safety of the State, Polignac had placarded Paris with four ordinances that changed the fundamental laws of France.

Ignorant of these events, Isidore delivered a fine speech about the capture of Algiers. "Not only has Your Majesty swept the Barbary pirates off the face of the ocean, but by this great and glorious victory Your Majesty has established the power of his dynasty for all time, in the dark continent of Africa as well as in Europe."

The King smiled, for until recently France had possessed but one foothold on African soil, the insignificant trading post of Senegal. "We shall pursue our conquests," he replied, "at home and abroad. At home we shall find the power to overcome all obstacles placed in our path by culpable manœuvres. There is no coming to terms with pirates anywhere."

He was so pleased with Isidore's address that he was prompted at first to confer a distinguished order on him. But on second thoughts he was deterred by the reminder that King Ferdinand of Naples had married his daughter Marie Amélie to his detested cousin, the Duke of Orleans, son of the preposterous Philippe Égalité. He could not forgive such a tactless misalliance. So he merely presented Isidore with a jewelled snuff-box.

The July revolution broke out on the morrow. Within three days Charles had to abdicate; within a week his detested cousin had received the crown. Louis Philippe took possession of the royal palace and, draped in the tricolour flag, received the applause of the people, while Charles took ship for England to end his days in exile.

But Isidore was not accredited to Charles's successor. Though the new Queen was a sister of his own sovereign he did not think it proper to pay his respects to the new Court. Moreover, he wished to return to Naples with the least possible delay, for he was desperately anxious to see little Hercules. He left Paris without setting foot in the Tuileries, a circumstance to which, according to the Neapolitans, Louis Philippe owed the prosperous beginning of his reign.

Impartial observers must admit that no king was ever more clearly the author of his downfall than

Charles X of France. But in Naples it was believed that he lost his throne through Isidore's embassy.

Isidore had been cured of sea voyages long ago—not that there was any danger of battles, but storms were still possible, and risk *per se* had ceased to appeal to him. Though mountains made him giddy, he preferred to cross the Alps and travel through Tuscany and the Papal states. His head was so full of Hercules and his future that he passed the intervening scenery with little patience and less attention. In Rome he naturally stopped to pay homage to Pope Pius VIII, who received him with all the honour due to his rank. Instead of offering him his foot to kiss, as with the common run of visitors, His Holiness extended his hand. Isidore embraced it with such fervour that the Pope felt faint. Three days later the Pope had passed away.

Chary of the pestilential vapours of the Campagna, Isidore left Rome immediately after his audience, hardly venturing to fall asleep on the journey. His carriage rattled on at full speed, with only the necessary halts for changing horses. The previous arrival of his courier gave the Prince's family time to assemble on the first-floor balcony. In their midst stood the nurse with the precious babe in her arms.

Thanks to the excellent glasses he had purchased in Paris, Isidore was able to see Hercules distinctly. He leaned from the carriage window and waved his hand.

The keen-eyed infant was quick to recognize him. Leaping for joy, he held out his little arms in an attempt, regardless of distance, to embrace him. So impetuous was the movement that he escaped from his nurse's clutch and, falling from the balcony, dashed his head against the hard pavement below.

Helen would have followed him, had not her husband restrained her. Isidore was greeted by her shrieks of despair on the doorstep. She had flung herself upon the little lifeless body and soon lay helplessly insensible beside it. When Luciano tried to lift her up in his arms, she sighed faintly and opened her eyes, but on seeing her father she uttered a loud moan. Her eyes closed again as if she had been struck by death.

It required the repeated efforts and all the ingenuity of the most celebrated doctor in Naples to bring her back to consciousness, after she had lain for days in this condition. What the doctor began was completed by her husband, who promised her that, with San Gennaro's aid, Hercules would soon be replaced by brothers, and by sisters perhaps as well. He rekindled her hopes with all the ardour of his philoprogenitive temperament, until she began to live again with eyes fixed on the future.

But Helen refused categorically to see her father. She trembled at the mere thought of him, as if he were a malignant spirit intent on her destruction. "Take me where I may never see him more," she cried. "Take me away! He must be in league with Satan." All her mother's arguments were unavailing: the bond between father and daughter was permanently severed.

Helen and Luciano left the Pizzofalcone palace and set up a separate household. Fortunately, they were drawn closer to each other by the birth of a second son.

Isidore was not allowed to approach him. For the time being it made little difference, since the shock of Hercules's death had unbalanced his mind. It seemed as if all his joy in life were buried with the child. His eyes stared blankly into space, more often than not incapable of recognition. In his lucid intervals, which were almost gloomier than his fits of abstraction, he told Margaret that it was no longer possible for him to ignore his condition of *jettatore*. He was being driven by an evil fate, and he felt personally responsible for the catastrophes of his past. "I am filled with the dread of terrible happenings, yet I have no power to avert them," he confessed. "Since my ill-starred birth I have been the blind instrument of a malevolent force. I had better end it all."

The mood of one moment gave no clue to the mood of the next, and the apathy of complete despair prevailed. Margaret devoted most of her time to the fruitless attempt to cheer him with reading, conversation and melodies on the harp. She could not induce him to set foot outside the palace. Day and night he would prowl through the rooms, muttering to himself with wild gesticulations. For hours on end he gazed at himself in a looking glass with implacable hatred. "This is tantamount to suicide," he thought. "I shall be killed by my own reflection." But nothing happened.

When a gust of wind blew the door of his study open, he imagined that the demon he had unwittingly obeyed all his life had finally come to see him. He fell on his knees and cried: "Oh, grant me love instead of fear and hatred! I am weary, and I am getting old. I implore you to set me free!"

The door stood wide open, but nobody was there. Then the door slammed. Isidore rushed to the same balcony from which Hercules had fallen and took a flying leap. He landed on top of two sleeping *lazzaroni*. The first died of concussion and the second broke a few ribs, but Isidore did not receive the slightest injury. Nobody had witnessed the accident, and the surviving victim was in no condition to remember how it had occurred. The Company of the Misericordia dealt with the corpse.

Since the impulse to survive is usually stronger than the impulse to perish, in yielding to the latter Isidore considered that he had tempted fate to the utmost. Obviously he was intended to survive. Henceforth it was his duty to live as cheerfully as possible. He owed this to Margaret, if not to himself. After such exceptional trials, he felt he had at last reached the point at which he could say with all freedom of conscience that he stood securely on his own feet. Yet he realized that he was like a loaded fire-arm which he must handle with the utmost caution, in the interest of all mankind.

He went into society as little as possible and remained at home on public festivals. At last he understood why acquaintances turned pale at the sight of him, and the feigned cordiality of those who groped furtively for an amulet or made that ridiculous gesture with the hand. He determined to out-manœuvre them by resorting to the same tactics, in the naïve hope that he would thereby render their measures more efficacious.

When he further examined the disasters which had all but overwhelmed him, he decided that his connection with them was fortuitous. They would have happened in any case. It was as if the crumbling ground beneath him had solidified.

He desired nothing from the past and he ceased to count on the future. The present would have to suffice him. Having renounced happiness, he grew moderately contented. And he became penetrated with a new sense of his own existence. "I cannot bear to think of being no more," he confided to Margaret. "Nay, it appears to me impossible that I should cease to exist."

EVER since Isidore understood, in all its crushing
implications, what sort of prejudice the masses
conceived against him, he began to adapt himself as
placidly as possible and make allowances for his
detractors, even for those who had cast the cruellest
aspersions. He had gained the faculty of seeing with
other people's eyes as well as with his own.

He forgave Helen her morbid aversion to him,
though this was his greatest chagrin after the death
of little Hercules. After all, there were many others,
including Margaret, who continued to live under the
same roof with him in the best of health. How was it

that they remained immune to his noxious influence?

He ventured to unbosom himself on the subject to Rosario, the venerable majordomo who had managed his family affairs for well nigh half a century. "You're not afraid of me like the rest, are you?" he asked him.

Old Rosario was taken aback. "Why should I have cause to fear Your Highness? My long record of service is untarnished, as everybody knows."

"Come, come. It is no use feigning ignorance of what all Naples says about me."

"I have always believed in minding my own business. What other folks may or may not say is no concern of mine."

"From henceforth you are to make it your concern. All Naples seems agreed that I have a terrifically potent Evil Eye. You have never heard of it? Granted. Yet you have been in the service of my family—for how many years?"

"Sixty-nine, Your Highness, considering that I was foster-brother to the late Prince, who was nourished by my mother's milk."

"You must have some special amulet in your possession. In that case, it would only be charitable to enlighten others. Such knowledge ought to be shared for the benefit of all."

"My sole amulet is my life-long devotion to the house of Pizzofalcone," said the old man, tears welling to his eyes. "I swear I possess no other. It has been put to many a trial, but none so severe as this. How could you think Rosario capable of listening to calumnies against Your Highness?"

"You must have raised a wall of deafness round you," said Isidore; "estimable, no doubt, but misguided. It has taken me a long time to discover what is the matter, a very long time. Now that I realize, I wish to be informed of every fresh incident that is credited to me by vulgar superstition. I am defenceless against these accusations unless I am warned in advance. I insist that you interrogate the servants and report to me day by day what they hear in the market-place. I shall then be able to take proper measures to repair the damage. When accused of causing death to anyone I am likely to have seen or come in contact with, I shall pay for Masses to be celebrated for their souls. In cases of financial or physical loss, I shall send anonymous letters of condolence to the sufferers, enclosing proportionate remittances of money. We shall have to economize. I have decided to give up coffee."

"I hope Your Highness will not confide this plan to others. If noised abroad, it will incite half the population to make claims on your generosity. Your Highness would soon be ruined, your legal heirs sacrificed to a pack of picaroons."

"So you knew it all the time, you old hypocrite! Half the population forsooth! Am I really held responsible for so many calamities?"

"Your Highness misapprehends me. I am a good Christian. I pay no attention to the gossip of idlers, with whom our beloved city abounds. It stands to reason that with the daily distribution of accidents Your Highness could have little or no connection.

But every Tom, Dick and Harry would rush forward with appeals for compensation when they saw a chance of financial gain and free Masses for dead relatives. The palace would be besieged by claimants of every species, and Your Highness would become involved in endless expenditure—a dangerous precedent! Furthermore, there is so much poverty in Naples that this would be an incentive to crime. People would be tempted to murder their next of kin and mangle themselves on your doorstep. It is so easy to put the blame—with all due respect—on Your Highness's 'fascination.' No secret can be kept for long in this city. The less fortunate would soon get wind of their anonymous benefactor. Take my advice, Your Highness, and change your mind!"

"I am touched by your solicitude, but my conscience is ill at ease. I refuse to be swaddled in darkness. You will report to me with your first bulletin this evening."

"This is contrary to my dearest principles. I have always discouraged gossip among the servants. It leads to scandal, and worse. Think twice, Your Highness!"

"Stop whimpering, and do as I bid you."

In a perverse and diffident way, Isidore had grown attached to the notion that he possessed the Evil Eye. He was shocked, but he was also intrigued, by the fatal authority with which he had been invested. Never would he bring himself to admit this, but the calamities which afflicted others excited emotions in him that were not entirely devoid of malicious pleasure. Finding himself so mysteriously involved in them, his curiosity became more subjective. The element of surprise, too, contained a certain piquancy.

Rosario's sense of loyalty should not be allowed to hamper his practical designs. These could only benefit the community, even if, as he said, the accidents could not all be charged to his account. For a second he almost wished that he wielded so formidable a power, but his natural goodness reproached him for it. He waited impatiently for Rosario's first bulletin, and the day seemed unusually long. When Rosario knocked at the door of his study, Isidore bounced from his chair and greeted him with unaccustomed eagerness. "Come in, my friend. Let us hear the latest. Am I due for a heavy indemnity?"

"Mercifully not, Your Highness."

"Proceed with the details at once."

"Item one: it is rumoured that a picture fell out of its frame this morning while you were passing Don Filippo Siviero's house in your carriage. Don Filippo was peeping out of the window—he seldom does aught else these days—when the picture crashed on his cranium. He has a bump, but nothing serious."

"What about the picture?"

"He claims that it is a valuable Salvator Rosa. There's a large rent in the canvas which will have to be repaired."

"It must have been predestined," said Isidore, not without a trace of vexation. "I was a considerable distance away; besides, my carriage is one of the fastest in Naples. The story will not hold water; it is too far-fetched."

"I rejoice to hear you say so, for I am of the same opinion," said Rosario.

"Well, what next?"

"Item two: Peppino the mason, who has been mending the roof, fell off his scaffolding soon after Your Highness went to ask how his work was progressing."

"There may be something in that. Was he badly injured?"

"He sprained his back, but he is tolerably well in other respects. It has nowise diminished his phenomenal thirst. We shall have to engage another mason, however, since Peppino refuses to carry on with his work. He declares it was Your Highness who caused him to stumble."

"What nonsense," said Isidore indignantly. "All the same, perhaps I did; the fellow may be right. But I swear it never crossed my mind at the time. I must be careful to avoid scaffolds in future. I'll pay his doctor's fee and compensate him for lost time. Make a note of it, Rosario. What next?"

"That is all for to-day."

Isidore looked disgruntled. "Hardly an impressive beginning. Only two accidents of the most trivial kind, mere bagatelles! I anticipated news more worthy of my reputation."

"How can Your Highness make light of it? It cuts me to the quick."

"I suppose I should be grateful to hear nothing worse. Are you sure that that is all?"

"Quite positive, Your Highness."

"Maintain your vigilance and sharpen your ears."

Isidore dismissed his factotum with a benevolent smile and opened a bulky folio bound in vellum which was lying on his desk. He had written on the title-page: "The Book of Bad Luck. Calamities commonly attributed to Prince Isidore Pizzofalcone." Now he wrote the date and beneath it a description of the accidents just related to him. The description did not flow from his pen too easily, but practice would make perfect. Eventually his style would improve and the narrative become inspired by the subject matter. Already he experienced something of an author's glow of pride.

Every evening Rosario returned with his report, and as his reserve broke down he too became interested in his assignment. From examining each incident academically, he proceeded to analyse it with a warmth of imagination and a wealth of gesture which astonished and delighted his master. He provided Isidore with a capital fund of entertainment.

Margaret visited Helen once a week and brought back good news of his grandchildren. Though his craving to see them was at times unbearable, he held himself aloof with a stoical self-control, never venturing in the vicinity of Torre del Greco, where Helen and Luciano had settled in a commodious villa.

"Do you think it would harm the children if I had their miniatures painted?" he asked Margaret. "You have given me excellent descriptions, but I should love to see what they look like all the same."

"You poor darling, of course you would! But you

know what Helen is, with her obsession. If I broach the subject openly she will never consent. It will have to be done on the sly."

Margaret succeeded, but when she brought Isidore the miniatures he forced himself to turn away. "I dare not look at them," he said with a shudder. "I'm afraid of what my eyes might do."

"How I wish you could get rid of this monstrous delusion! Take courage, dear. I'll assume the responsibility myself."

But Isidore's gaze was fixed in an opposite direction, and its expression was such that she feared again for his sanity. He did not shed a tear, but the haggard face betrayed so hopeless, so profound, so sublime a sorrow, that he appeared to her a being of a nature superior to humanity. Margaret bowed her head in silent compassion.

Apart from this episode, she noticed that his spirits had recovered their accustomed tone. The dark pressure upon them seemed to have been removed. He was even pleased to hear that Helen's first husband had been reinstated as a male. Following Helen's example, Carlino had married again, and the union had been blessed with two sons and a daughter. Isidore sent them gifts of coral horns. A new sense of social community with the world about him, and a gleam of human interest, if not of enjoyment, had begun to reanimate him. Now that he was bald he had bought himself a wig, and the coalition of this with his eye-glasses and snuff-box was generally regarded as lethal.

Margaret continued to be absorbed by her charities among the poor, who treasured her smiles as much as the soup and soap she distributed. She was esteemed by all as a saint, and could walk through the foulest slums in perfect safety. It was largely owing to her representations at Court that a Sanitary Commission was formed to improve the public hygiene, and she urged Isidore to give it his fullest support. So munificent were his contributions, above those of any other citizen, that the members of the Commission wished to show their gratitude. After an uproarious session, they decided to elect him their honorary Chairman. This would be a graceful gesture and noncommittal, since his actual presence would not be required at their meetings.

The ruling members called on him in a body to give him notice of this appointment. Isidore professed himself gratified, but his alert eye could not fail to detect the usual tokens of nervousness. With broad hints and devious compliments, they led him to understand that it would be superfluous for their honorary Chairman, amid so many responsibilities, to waste valuable time at their ordinary meetings. "The permanent goodwill of Your Highness is all we require," was the gist of their perorations.

Isidore appreciated their delicacy, and he was amused to observe how strenuously they persevered with the familiar gesture. For the horned hand, whether inside the pocket or behind the back, was plainly discernible. He looked forward to presiding at their conferences, he said; he was never too busy to devote himself to the common weal.

"It's quite simple," muttered one member. "He need not be told until the meeting is over."

Isidore persuaded them to partake of some refreshment, and they discussed their future plans for plague-prevention.

"I am deeply honoured by the confidence you have all shown in electing me your Chairman," said Isidore. "I shall try to prove worthy of it. The Sanitary Commission has a great deal of work ahead. Though I doubt the recurrence of any plague, it is wise to be prepared."

Recently Rosario's bulletin had begun to pall. The assessment of accidents had been exceedingly low. Isidore realized, with mixed emotions, that his reputation was waning. On the one hand, he was relieved; on the other, his sense of the dramatic and his newly developed pride in authorship were disappointed. A week passed, a fortnight, a month, yet the incidents Rosario related were of a uniform banality. He was bored by having to chronicle miscarriages and carriage accidents, and he was ready to welcome a change. "The Book of Bad Luck" would never be a work of art at this rate.

All too soon the change occurred, and Isidore regretted his impatience. The day after he was elected to the Sanitary Commission, Rosario reported that cholera had broken out and that His Highness was held responsible by the great majority. Isidore protested rather lamely and tendered his resignation to the Commission. But by then several of its most active members had succumbed and the others had dispersed in panic.

The epidemic spread with galloping violence. Whole families perished in a day, and the list of victims became so interminable that Isidore could not find room for them in his book. He was forced to give it up; the task would have required a regiment of secretaries.

The Neapolitans had always been excitable, and the present holocaust, aggravated by a thousand hideous rumours, drove the population to a delirium of despair. Many died from the effects of sheer terror. Huddled together in airless hovels and narrow alleys, wailing for San Gennaro to deliver them and wondering whose turn would come next, they were like bleating lambs branded for slaughter. Only the religious fraternities showed signs of life. Processions of priests and bare-footed friars and penitents in sackcloth and ashes flocked from church to church or staggered with statues of saints through the streets, imploring the mercy of Heaven.

But the fear of contagion soon put an end to all assemblies. Vast areas of the city—wherever the plague had been most virulent—were sealed off with crosses and the words, "Lord have mercy upon us." No one

went in or out of these infected enclosures, the abodes of hunger and thirst and lamentation. The relentless sun blazed down on the survivors, who barely breathed beside the bloated corpses of their nearest and dearest, waiting with parched tongues and inflamed eyeballs to share their fate.

Ever and anon the brooding silence was torn by shrieks or shattered by the tinkling of a bell. This signified that a priest was carrying the Last Sacrament to another moribund creature. Soon this was also forbidden. The dying writhed without hope of consolation; once dead, they were piled on top of one another without ceremony. During the night they were given a secret, hasty burial. The police regulations ordained that all corpses were to be cast into a special hole in the cholera cemetery, to be destroyed by quicklime.

Isidore refused to believe that he alone was responsible for this contagion. Rosario had told him that there were others reputed to be *jettatori* in Naples. He decided to investigate them. It would only be just to make them share the burden. He would invite them to a rally in his palace, to discuss ways and means of halting the epidemic. If they refused to enter into a friendly alliance with him, he would direct all his influence in opposition to theirs. It was a bold, ambitious scheme. Ultimately he would either suppress them or be suppressed. His new mission was to liberate Naples from the Evil Eye.

He sent Margaret to join Helen and Luciano at Torre del Greco. Their villa was about fifteen miles from Naples, and the air from the sea, filtered through a forest of aromatic pines, was purer and less liable to contamination. Margaret was reluctant to leave Isidore, but he insisted. He owed it to Naples to remain there and fight the plague. For himself he was utterly fearless.

The list of Isidore's colleagues, as he called them in jest, was longer than he had suspected. Rosario secured over twenty names, among them several monks, a renowned surgeon and a shoemaker. But none of these would accept the role thrust upon him. As for Isidore's proposal to hold a rally, one and all rejected it with indignation. His courteous invitations to co-operate were torn up with insulting comments; his messengers were abused and, in several cases, assaulted and driven out of the house.

Apparently Isidore was the only *jettatore* in Naples who recognized his moral obligations. He was discouraged but not defeated. Regardless of the appalling spectre that stalked the streets, he went in person to appeal to the most enlightened of his reputed rivals. He fared no better than his messengers. The contagion had made them truculent and hostile. Despite his wealth and rank, they refused to see him.

The sole exception was Canon Ojori, whose audience with King Ferdinand I was generally believed to have hastened that monarch's decease. The Canon was at least polite.

"How brave of Your Highness to come and visit me!" he exclaimed. "This is a pleasant surprise. I have seen nobody for a fortnight. What can I do for you? Pray sit down. You are looking tired."

"Not at all, not at all, my dear Canon. There cannot be much risk in one *jettatore* visiting another. Your Reverence is no doubt familiar with my reputation?"

The Canon laughed heartily. "The only risk I know is the prevalence of cholera. Are you not afraid of the contagion?"

"Not for myself, but for others. The extent of its ravages is spectacular. I came to see you in the hope that we might devise a means to combat it together. They hold us responsible, you know."

"Mortal disease is outside my province. I leave that to the physicians. My concern as a priest is with the human soul. I can assure you that that is ample."

"But as a *jettatore*, Your Reverence must admit . . ."

The Canon drew himself up and said, "I admit nothing of the kind. *Jettatura*'s all nonsense. Death and disease are no rarities, and in times like these there is apt to be greater deception and self-deception. The ignorant infect one another with superstitions as with cholera, and their feeble minds reflect the nightmares of their neighbours."

"You would be astonished to learn how many deaths and diseases have been attributed to both of us. Are you not aware that you are credited with the Evil Eye? The dismal knowledge has been forced upon me."

"I should feel flattered," said the Canon with a quizzical smile, "that you consider me as a peer with equal powers. But I must deny it at the cost of seeming impolite. Our eyes are no more deleterious than anyone else's, though it does no harm to let fools think so. Personally, I have had many an opportunity to be grateful. The reputation has served me as a protection against bores. In consequence, I have been allowed to pursue my meditations in peace. I would advise Your Highness to view it in the same light."

Canon Ojori's gentle black eyes were focused kindly on Isidore. They were opaque and dusty, like ink-spots dried with sand, but their expression was benevolent and resigned. The world and its delusions were to him as the lost continent of Atlantis. Isidore leaned back in his chair and sank into a torpor, from which he could hear the Canon's voice emerge like a rustling of dead leaves. He was slipping into a state of indescribable indolence. Though he wanted to shut his eyes, he seemed to have lost the capacity. For a period which seemed infinitely protracted his will ceased to act on his body. He felt paralysed, while the Canon kept staring at him with his exasperating smile.

The Canon did not appear to notice his discomfiture. At last, with a shrug of the shoulders, he said: "No; I regret I cannot help Your Highness in this matter. I wish it lay within my power. Perhaps it lies in yours, but give me leave to doubt it. These epidemics are due to natural causes. They are scourges which it is reasonable to suppose are sent from on high. We are in God's hands: nothing can happen without His permission and all will end happily for those who love Him."

With a tremendous effort, Isidore rose to take leave of his host. He did not feel himself. He had suffered pain at various times, but this was different; a misery which crept through every joint and muscle of his body. He was suddenly very frightened. Was this a foretaste of cholera, perhaps of death? But his brain was still lucid. He managed to reach the door, walking with supreme labour, as if his legs did not belong to him. The Canon seized his hand, which was stiff and cold, and asked anxiously if he were indisposed.

Isidore could only answer with a groan. For an instant he tottered; he was growing weaker and dizzier under the Canon's gentle gaze. "Dear me!" sighed the priest, "people will soon be saying that I put the Evil Eye on you!" He offered him smelling salts and sprinkled some disinfectant on the Prince's coat. "Are you feverish?" he asked.

Isidore answered faintly that he had no idea what was the matter with him. He had never felt like this before, overpowered by an unfathomable fatigue.

"I imagine it must be the consequence of over-exertion," said the Canon. "Your Highness should go to the country for a rest and change of air. I would do so myself, but that my duties detain me in Naples."

"So do mine," muttered Isidore. He stumbled and would have fallen if the Canon had not escorted him to his carriage.

"I trust this distemper will soon pass. I shall compose a special prayer for your recovery," said the Canon earnestly.

"Amen—I mean, thank you!" said Isidore, drawing in his breath through his teeth, as men do in pain. Instinctively he made the gesture of the horned hand as he sank among the cushions of his chariot.

The horses tossed their manes and bolted. Kicking and plunging, they thundered through the streets in a

frenzy of terror. The carriage rattled after them with hiccups of protest, the only mobile element in a petrified panorama—for the streets were deserted, as if the citizens had fled in a mass migration. Isidore felt he was in a drunken hearse. He saw the coachman as a skeleton whipping up his horses to the cemetery. He shouted at him to stop, but the carriage jolted on remorselessly.

When at last the carriage halted, the coachman had to carry him out, for he was unable to move. He was put to bed, and Naples was searched for a doctor. Half the medical profession had expired or run away, but eventually a young apothecary who practised medicine was found. His diagnosis was not very illuminating. Perhaps he lacked experience; perhaps he was intimidated by his patient. He declared that there was nothing amiss except some slight derangement of the digestive organs, for which he accordingly wrote a prescription.

Livid and immobile though Isidore lay, there was a twinkle in his eyes. Suddenly he trembled all over in a convulsion of laughter which brought on an attack of coughing, so prolonged that he seemed in the throes of death. With each wheeze his breathing grew fainter; he was bathed in perspiration.

The apothecary turned pale and examined his pulse again. It gave grounds for apprehension, he asserted, but this was not a cholera case. He wrote another prescription.

Isidore was gasping for air; his contracted fingers clawed at the coverlet. His face was contorted, his nostrils were pinched, yet the twinkle in his eyes persisted; it might have been a trick of light, a flickering beam from the window. He tried to speak, but the words melted in foam on his lips. Rosario sent a message urging the Princess to hasten to his bedside.

After twenty-four hours the apothecary's prescriptions had failed to produce the slightest impression on Isidore's disease. He was just as faint, if not fainter. At the sight of Margaret he rallied all his strength to speak and collapsed in a coma. Margaret was so alarmed that she insisted on a consultation with an older physician who had accompanied her from Torre del Greco. He examined the patient without a word, looking graver every minute.

Except his lips and eyes, Isidore could not move. The eyes followed both attendants with an expression of mockery; the lips twitched over yellow teeth like the silent keys of a piano. Each practitioner felt his pulse in turn. They nodded in unison and withdrew to the library to discuss his case. Margaret, from the adjoining room, heard their voices rise in altercation. The apothecary kept shouting, "How can you prove it? You must prove it scientifically."

The senior said, "It's a question of experience. You must take my word for it. I was in this profession before you were born or thought of."

"You're senile," shouted the junior. "A gibbering survival from the Middle Ages."

"Silence, you jackanapes!"

There was the sound of a scuffle, and Margaret entered the library. In defence of their theories, the doctors were slapping and kicking each other. The apothecary had drawn a stiletto. Margaret made a gesture of helplessness. "Where am I to turn?" she exclaimed. "The Prince is dying. You're the only people who can do anything to save him. Is this how you propose to do it?"

Their arms fell to their sides, and they bowed apologies.

"We are getting nowhere," said the apothecary. "My venerable colleague maintains that His Highness has been bewitched by an Evil Eye."

"Pardon me," said the physician. "I shall state my

own view of the case another time, preferably in your absence. I regret that by my science I can accomplish nothing."

Margaret addressed him with despairing vehemence. "I was counting on you," she wailed. "Have you nothing to suggest?"

"No natural disease exhibits such symptoms," he answered. "This kind of paralysis can only be arrested by exorcism. I advise you to send for the nearest priest. His prayers will achieve more than any medicine."

"Mere mumbo-jumbo," said his rival. "Since my services are unnecessary, I shall retire." But he was seized by griping pains before he left the house, and within a few hours he was raving with cholera fever.

Margaret had always been sceptical about the Evil Eye, but rather than attempt nothing she sent for the nearest priest.

Padre Ziviello came ringing a little bell. Being stone deaf, he imagined that the patient was another cholera victim. He was clad in a dingy cassock, and when his cadaverous form advanced towards the canopied bed where Isidore was lying, even Margaret had the impression that he was the herald of death. The doctor took the priest aside and shouted down his ear that he had to deal with an insidious case of *jettatura*, for which exorcism was the only remedy. Padre Ziviello nodded: he had often dealt with cases of a similar nature.

Isidore was ashen pale, but his dilated eyes still followed every gesture. His room was fumigated with incense, and holy water was sprinkled on the sheets.

169

The doctor kept his hand on the patient's pulse, while the entire household congregated at the foot of the bed and repeated the prayers intoned by Padre Ziviello. The prayers were interminable, and being couched in monkish Latin their meaning was far from intelligible to all; but everybody supplied with lung power what he lacked in comprehension. The doctor was swaying to and fro, as if in rhythm to the chanting. Suddenly he lurched and plumped down with a thud, still clutching Isidore's pulse and dragging him some distance along the floor. Isidore was promptly carried back to bed. He had not been hurt; on the contrary, a speck of colour had returned to his cheeks.

The doctor remained prostrate. Margaret emptied her scent-bottle over him; his jacket was unbuttoned; but it was soon apparent that his heart had stopped beating. All knelt again while Padre Ziviello recited the orisons for the dead.

At this point Isidore's hands began to quiver. He was making signs that he wished to write, but nobody could understand them. His lips were twitching in a violent effort to expel some pent-up words. He gnawed them till they bled; he munched and chewed his saliva, while everybody gathered round him. Eventually, with a spasm that rocked the bed from side to side, he whispered audibly: "Bring me the Book of Bad Luck."

In the meantime, the priest was beginning to betray the same symptoms as the doctor, and in the midst of his prayers he swooned, flopping and folding over like a wounded crow. This third collapse set up a general howl. The maidservants ran out of the room. After slamming the door, they continued to run in all directions, some upstairs and some downstairs. Several locked themselves up in their attics and screamed out of the windows for help, as if the palace had caught fire. Needless to say, the streets remained deserted; the women screamed themselves hoarse in vain.

Only Margaret retained her composure. Since most of the servants were behaving like frightened chickens in a barnyard, she decided to nurse Isidore herself. She held him in her arms and did everything possible to keep him warm.

By slow degrees his head was sinking into his body, as if overcome by a supernatural pressure. When Rosario brought the book and writing materials he was horrified by his master's deterioration. Not only had he shrunk into a shrivelled gnome, but his head had sunk so low that its crown was scarcely perceptible above his shoulders. His face looking forward with lurid eyes, lolled against the collar-bone and could not be kept in position, unless supported by Margaret and Rosario in turn, since both of them found it an extremely heavy burden. In this posture he languished during the night, unable to swallow food, either liquid or solid.

Margaret sent an urgent message to Helen, begging her to forgive her father on his deathbed. But Helen never came. Isidore's eyes drifted hither and thither without resting. The twinkle had left them; the lids began to droop, and a film was settling over the dwindling pupils. At last they seemed crushed under the dome of his forehead, like that of a Roman statesman made of marble. He expired so peacefully that neither Margaret nor Rosario, who kept vigil, were aware of the moment of his passing to a better life. There was a grateful smile on his countenance when Margaret closed his eyes.

Isidore had expressed a wish to be buried beside little Hercules in the family vault. He was interred accordingly, on a beautiful summer day. Not a cloud disturbed the Chinese porcelain serenity of the sky. The mourners were few, since so many who might have mourned for the mere pleasure of it had perished in the epidemic.

Canon Ojori presided at the funeral, and he felt inspired to pronounce an eloquent oration, which was subsequently published at Margaret's expense. It is now a literary curiosity and a rare collector's item. The text was chosen from the Ninety-first Psalm: "Thou shalt not be afraid for the terror by night; nor for the arrow that flieth by day; nor for the pestilence that walketh in darkness; nor for the destruction that wasteth at noonday. A thousand shall fall at thy side, and ten thousand at thy right hand; but it shall not come nigh thee. Only with thine eyes shalt thou behold and see the reward of the wicked."

All concurred that it was a soul-stirring tribute to one *jettatore* from another. Prince Isidore Pizzofalcone was depicted in all the actions of a life-time as an instrument of Heaven and a paragon of citizenship deserving the pride of Naples, ever modest, humane and self-sacrificing. While his singular rank and fortune might have led him into worldly temptations, he had resisted them heroically, etc.

As soon as Isidore was buried, an exceptional gust of wind blew over the entire city from the sea. It was short and sharp, and in the meantime the bells that were tolling for Isidore cracked in the belfry; the cupola of the Pizzofalcone Chapel toppled down, and the vault caved in with a subterranean rumble that was heard for many miles. The burning tapers on the altar set fire to what remained of Isidore's mortuary. After raging for several hours, the flames were extinguished by a torrential shower as abrupt as the previous blast. The last embers burned themselves out towards sunset. Rosario and a few stalwart dependents remained raking among the ashes, but little had survived the conflagration.

Certain it was that the cholera abated from the hour of Isidore's death. Naples awoke from its nightmares and danced in the sun, in a dazzled rapture at finding itself alive. Music returned to the labyrinthine streets, with its myriad accompaniments animal, vegetable and mineral; music returned to the grottoes where the sirens swam, and to the blue and gold mosaics of the bay. In the fishing villages along the coast the purr and pulse of life grew clamorous as of old; fresh blood plunged singing through the city's arteries. Eyes peeped through shutters at siesta-time with desire instead of terror; fans fluttered without fear of wafting infectious effluvia. Grand opera was revived at the San Carlo; plumed cavalcades caracoled along the Corso again. For the Unmentionable Prince, the kindest and deadliest of *jettatori*, had made his valediction permanent. Though history may repeat itself, it has not repeated his like in Naples or elsewhere, so far as I know.

To me he remains the most fascinating of fascinators. Perhaps I have fallen beneath his spell to the extent of overrating his achievements. Perhaps I have fallen too deeply altogether. . . . Hey, presto, where is my coral horn? Decidedly it has required some temerity to pen these pages, but at least it has been a labour of sympathy verging on love.

Printed in Great Britain by
The Camelot Press Ltd., London and Southampton